MAVERICK
HERITAGE

**Center Point
Large Print**

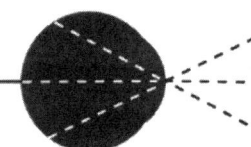

**This Large Print Book carries the
Seal of Approval of N.A.V.H.**

MAVERICK HERITAGE

Roe Richmond

CENTER POINT LARGE PRINT
THORNDIKE, MAINE

The text of this Large Print edition is unabridged.
In other aspects, this book may
vary from the original edition.
Printed in the United States of America
on permanent paper.
Set in 16-point Times New Roman type.

ISBN: 978-1-61173-436-2

Library of Congress Cataloging-in-Publication Data

Richmond, Roe.
  Maverick heritage / Roe Richmond. — Large print ed.
    p. cm. — (Center Point large print edition)
  ISBN 978-1-61173-436-2 (lib. bdg. : alk. paper)
  1. Large type books. I. Title.
PS3535.I424M38 2012
813'.54—dc23
                                            2012004304

For Mother

MAVERICK HERITAGE

Chapter I

Cordell cut out another calf and drove it into the chute, where the last one scrambled up bawling and bucked away, the smell of scorched hide mingling with the hot dust, heated iron and sweat of men and horses. Cordell's rawhide riata flickered out, caught the calf's forelegs and threw it, as the slate-colored pony skidded to an abrupt stiff-legged stop. Tannehill promptly pinned the frantic wiry little creature in the dirt and laid on the iron with a firm expert hand. The animal snorted and struggled in panic, bellowing with the shock of pain, as Cordell shook his loop free and reeled it in. Tannehill released the calf and watched it go bounding into the corral.

"I hope we aren't gettin' any Hatchet stock," Tannehill said, grinning up at the rider through the sunshot haze of dust.

"That'd be too bad, Tan," agreed Cordell soberly, wheeling his mount away to repeat the process.

Spring roundup was about finished on the Delsing spread. That was the last bunch of calves out there now. The Delsings—father, son and daughter—were holding the gather, while Cordell did the cutting and roping, and Tannehill attended to the branding. It was one of the small layouts on Wagon Mound, worked mainly by the family. Cordell and Tannehill were the only extra hands at present, and they would be leaving as soon as the roundup was over. Ash Cordell never stayed long in any one place, and Tannehill was content to follow wherever the other went.

It was this thought that troubled Laura Delsing, as she drifted back and forth on her bay mare, helping keep the herd intact, and watching the two men at work. They could have qualified as top hands on any of the big ranches, but they preferred to work for the smaller outfits—when they worked. Her eyes lingered particularly upon the big rangy man topping the blue roan with the gray mane and tail. It was a pleasure to watch the effortless grace and flawless precision of rider and horse, moving in perfect coordination with never a false or wasted motion, none of the flourishes that showy cowhands indulged in. But Laura Delsing's admiration went deeper than that.

She knew Cordell was going, and nothing she could say or do would hold him. He had stayed on the Double-D longer than he remained at most places, through the beef roundup last fall, the mild Southwest winter, and now the spring roundup of young stock. That, she knew, was because of her, and probably it was a tribute, but it was not enough for Laura.

Dan Delsing, her father, was worried too, aware

of her feeling for Cordell. He knew that she was going to be hurt, and he had warned her about it. Slumped in his saddle, wide shoulders and stocky form sagging, Dan watched Cordell with a tired sun-squinted frown. He liked Ash about as well as any man he knew, but that did not alter the fact that Ash Cordell was a fiddle-footed incurable drifter, no man for any girl to fall in love with. I should have sent him along last fall, Dan Delsing thought. I might have known. They're the best men I ever had riding for me, but I shouldn't have hired them on at all.

Young Fritz Delsing, seventeen, with sunny blond hair under his hat, was following the movements of Cordell with absolute hero-worship in his bright blue eyes. All he asked was to grow up to be like Ash Cordell. And the long, lean, drawling Tannehill was second only to Ash, in the boy's mind. It sure was lucky that those two had come along, he reflected gratefully. And he hated to think of their leaving as much as Laura did, if for a different reason. Sometimes Fritz resented his sister because she hung around and dragged Ash off with her. He knew Ash would rather be talking man-talk with Tan and him, but of course Ash was too polite to hurt a girl's feelings.

Fritz was growing impatient now with the tedious business of holding the little herd, and he called out: "Hey, Ash! How about me takin' a few of 'em in?"

"Why, sure, Fritz," said Cordell. "I was gettin' tired anyway. Go right ahead, son."

The boy unlimbered his rope and booted his pony in to cut out a heifer, and Cordell started easing out around the bunched stock toward Laura. But Tannehill yelled from the branding pen: "Cord, you wanta spell me for a stretch? I've eaten about all the dust and smoke my delicate stomach can stand."

"Be right in, Tan," said Cordell, turning back and trailing Fritz as the boy hazed his calf into the chute. It was just as well if he kept working and didn't spend too much time with Laura, thought Cordell. It was getting hard to talk to her lately, with both of them thinking about the imminent separation. This was one time that Cordell cursed the eternal fever of restlessness that possessed him and wouldn't let him settle down anywhere. The Double-D had been like home these past months. The Delsings were a fine family, and it had been very comfortable and pleasant there. But the urge to move was on him now, and Cordell knew from experience there was no use in fighting it. Not even for a girl like Laura.

Fritz missed his first cast completely, and caught but one leg on the second try, much to his disgust. Tannehill wrestled the animal down in the weltering dust, planting the iron and loosening the kid's rope. "I'll get the next critter clean, Tan," promised Fritz. "Musta been kinda nervous on that one."

"Sure, Fritz," drawled Tannehill. "You got to get into the swing of it, that's all. Watchin' Cord's no great help to a young hand."

Cordell, about to step down, sank back into the leather and stared off across the sunburnt surface of Wagon Mound into the southeast. Out toward the needle-sharp columns of the Spires, a dust cloud was rising saffron in the sunlight.

"Company comin', Tan," murmured Cordell.

Tannehill walked to the rail where his gun-belt hung, and buckled it about his slender hips, tying down the bottom of the holster. "We got time to finish 'em up, Cord?"

Cordell estimated quickly and smiled. "With a man like me on the irons, I reckon so. You and the kid keep 'em comin', Tan." He swung out of the saddle, and Tannehill stepped into it.

"You sure this crowbait cayuse'll hold up, Cord? If it does, the kid and I'll bury you in young beef."

Cordell rinsed his mouth and drank from the water bucket, looked to the irons in the fire, and waited for the calves. Fritz roped and threw his second one with deft dispatch, and Tannehill choused another in and spilled it at Cordell's feet. They came fast after that, almost too fast at times, and Cordell was soaked with sweat in the swirling heat-laden dust. The bunch outside dwindled rapidly, and Dan Delsing sent Laura in to the ranch house. Young Fritz was whooping it up, having the time of his life, and Tannehill was laughing and shouting with him, heaping jovial abuse upon Cordell's dripping bronze head.

They had completed the job, and were waiting at rest, as the incoming riders approached. There were five of them, and even at a distance there was something that marked them apart from ordinary cowhands or cattlemen. A fighting-cock arrogance in the way they rode, an aggressive warlike aspect about them. Some of the Garriott gunhands from Hatchet, the largest spread in the Carikaree Valley, Ash Cordell recognized at once, and the old hatred for everything pertaining to Hatchet and the Garriotts stirred deep and bitter within him.

"Go in and help your mother and sister, Fritz," ordered Dan Delsing.

The boy shook his tow-head stubbornly, a pleading look on his thin flushed face. "Please, Dad. There's five of *them.*"

"It'll be all right, Dan," said Cordell gently. "There won't be any trouble here."

He could identify the individual riders as they drew closer, and Cordell smiled with grave amusement at the surprise and disappointment they showed on finding Tannehill and himself there with the Delsings. Neither of the Garriott boys, Gene or Kyler, was in the party. Talboom

14

seemed to be the leader, a tall lank man with a knobby beaked face, pitted with pockmarks. Skowron, short and squat, bloated and red of face, with pig-like eyes, was evidently second in command.

Eakins was a small warped figure with a large chew of tobacco lumping his wizened cheek. Blodwen, a giant gone grossly fat, looked too heavy for any horse to carry, even the huge black he straddled this afternoon. Thorner was young, well built, darkly and incongruously handsome in that ugly group, cool and debonair despite the blazing heat. They all wore two guns and had carbines in their saddle-boots. Reining up near the corrals, they sat their horses and stared down at the three dismounted men and the boy before them. The silence stretched out thin, and the tension grew intolerable.

"Well, what do you want?" Ash Cordell asked evenly at last.

"Nothin' from you," Talboom said, studying the newly branded calves. "Your herd's growin', Delsing. You got a lot of young stuff."

"It's all mine," Dan Delsing said, standing square and solid with thumbs hooked into his gun-belt.

"I wonder some," mused Talboom. "You Wagon Mound nesters always swung a long rope."

"Watch your talk, mister," warned Dan. "This is no nester outfit, and you danged well know

15

it! I got a legal claim here and my brand's registered."

Talboom smiled, a crooked gash across his bony pocked features. "Times change. I suppose some of you bobtailed outfits are legitimate nowadays. But to Carikaree cattlemen, Wagon Mound'll always mean honyonkers with long ropes, crooked runnin' irons and alterin' markin' knives."

"Did old Gurney send you?" Cordell broke in, anger fretting his impatience. "What the devil do you want here anyway? Sing your piece and drift along, Talboom."

The Hatchet men looked at him hard and cold but with a certain grudging respect. They knew Cordell and Tannehill, and they hadn't expected to find them still at the Double-D. The ragged-pants fly-by-night spreads on Wagon Mound seldom had riders of this caliber. Generally they were dull-eyed, heavy-handed farmers, family men who didn't want to fight and die in front of their womenfolks and young ones. Downtrodden failures, broken by hardship and poverty, who could be bullied and pushed around. Dan Delsing was a different type, however, while Cordell and Tannehill were not to be crossed unless you were ready for a finish fight.

"Gurney Garriott's kept you alive for quite a spell, Cord," said Talboom mildly. "You never did appreciate what old Gurney's done for you, and your brother and sister too. But the boys, Kyler more'n Gene, don't seem to share them senti-ments of Gurney's. The Carikaree ain't goin' to be any country for you, Cord, when old Gurney turns Hatchet over to his boys."

"That's my worry, Tal," said Cordell calmly. "You've had your say; now slope along out. This is a workin' ranch here."

"We'll travel in our own time, Cord," said Talboom.

Eakins spat tobacco juice at horseflies on the corral bar. "We're checkin' Wagon Mound brands, hopin' we don't find any altered Hatchets." He winked slyly at young Fritz, who scowled back at him.

"You won't in my herd," Dan Delsing told them flatly. "Unless you plant 'em there."

Skowron chuckled and shook his oversized, neckless head. "Nesters is all right till they start growin' big, actin' like real ranchers."

Blodwen moaned and wiped his fat perspiring countenance. "Let's dust along, Tal," he mumbled through the neckerchief.

"I'll maybe see you around sometime, Cord," said Tonk Thorner, a pleasant smile on his good-looking dark face, a reckless hungry light in his intense black eyes.

"Why, sure, Tonk," agreed Ash Cordell easily.

Tannehill stood slim and whiplike, contempt plain on his smooth lean face. "Long on talk and

17

short on action," he drawled. "Like 'most all the two-gun men you see hereabouts."

Tonk Thorner switched his dark gaze to Tannehill. "Maybe you and me'll meet up too, Tan."

"It's a small world," conceded Tannehill. "I just hope you're in front of me, Tonk, instead of at my back."

With an effort Thorner curbed his anger. "Don't you worry none about that, brother!"

The Hatchet riders loped away deeper into the wide seared tableland of Wagon Mound, the three men and the boy watching them for a space before gathering up equipment and leading their horses toward the ranch. The sun was sinking blood-red toward the massive Madrelinos in the west, and the mountain horizon was stained with brilliant changing colors in which flame predominated, while the shadows lengthened blue, gray and lavender on the plain.

"It's a good thing you boys were here," Dan Delsing said.

"Aw, they ain't so much, them five!" said young Fritz scornfully.

"Watch your grammar, son," his father reproved him wearily.

Ash Cordell smiled and cuffed the boy's bright blond head. "You're all right, Fritz. You stood up to them good, boy."

"Bunch of scrubs," Tannehill murmured in his

slow soft voice. "If they'd known we was here, Cord, they might've sent some of the good ones. Kyler Garriott himself, Hodkey, Laidlaw, and Hamrick."

"Never seen that Hodkey," mused Cordell.

"He don't hang around the home range much, but they say he's hellfire with a six-gun."

Double-D lay before them in the sparse shade of cottonwoods, feathered with delicate new green leaves, quiet, peaceful and homelike in the fading afternoon. Cordell felt a sudden pang at the thought of leaving here. He wondered if Laura had been watching that scene at the corrals, and smiled gravely to himself. If he knew that girl, she'd not only been watching; she'd had a rifle lined on the Hatchet crew all through it. And if anything had started out there, Laura would have dropped a couple of them, at least.

The ranch house was long and low, simple and trim, a clean frame structure reinforced at the corners with log and adobe. There was a small log bunkhouse, a large frame barn, and the usual jumble of sheds, corrals and out-buildings. Nothing elaborate or pretentious, but the Delsing layout was neat and utilitarian, well kept and friendly, built to last as a permanent home. Dan was a good cattleman, and his brand was growing constantly.

Cordell hoped it wouldn't grow so much that Hatchet would feel obliged to move against

Double-D and wipe it out. Hatchet had done that to other promising layouts on Wagon Mound, the Woodlees', for instance. Old Gurney Garriott owned the whole eastern end of the Carikaree Basin, the richest grasslands in the area, but he was a man obsessed with the idea of creating an empire for himself. There was no satisfying a greed like Garriott's. There could never be enough land and cattle and money for old Gurney, and Kyler Garriott was filled with the same driving, grasping ambition.

Orphaned in early childhood, Ash and his brother Clement and his sister Sue Ellen had been taken in by the Garriotts and brought up on Hatchet. In spite of this, Ash Cordell hated that outfit with a bitter undying hatred, bone-deep and utterly beyond his control.

"Cord, you and Tan go ahead and get cleaned up," Dan Delsing offered. "Fritz and I'll take care of the horses."

"You goin' swimmin', boys?" asked Fritz. "I'll be right with you in a jiffy."

The spring rains had increased the water in the irrigation ditch that bordered the ranch site, scarcely enough for much swimming but sufficiently for bathing. Dan and other homesteaders had dug the ditch from Bittersweet Creek, which flowed from the Shellerdine Mountains on the north, watering the western margin of Wagon Mound, and wound on southward to its junction with the Carikaree near the town of Cadmus Flats, centrally located in the vast lowland trough. When there was adequate water, the swim was a daily ritual that Cordell and Tannehill enjoyed almost as much as Fritz did.

Afterward, glowing clean and dressed in fresh clothes, they all sat down to one of Mrs. Delsing's delicious suppers at the large table in the ranch house, fragrant with the aroma of cooking from the immaculate kitchen. Mrs. Delsing, a handsome woman who had grown a bit gray and put on weight in recent years, bustled about trying to wait on everyone, a fond smile on her comely plump face, flushed rosily from the cookstove.

"Well, I suppose you boys are still set on ridin' off," Dan said, broad and stolid at the head of the gingham-covered board. "Reckon there's nothin' we can do to hold you up."

Cordell's smile was somber. "If any place could hold me, it'd be this one, Dan."

"We sure enjoyed winterin' here," Tannehill drawled. "*I* wouldn't mind summerin' here too, but this wild Indian I travel with—come spring, he's got to see what's over the hill, across the plain, on the other side of the mountains."

"It must be Mom's cooking that might hold you, Ash," chided Laura gently.

"Not altogether, but it would help a lot," Cordell admitted. "There are other things, Laura. They all add up to a mighty fine place for a man to make his home."

"I wish I was ridin' with you," Fritz said wistfully.

"A couple more years and you'd do to take along, Fritz," said Cordell.

"I'm almost eighteen, Ash. You ran away from Hatchet and hit it on your own when you was that age."

Cordell laughed softly. "I was born wild and tough and ornery, Fritz. Even so, I wouldn't have left a place like this."

"You'd leave any place, Ash, and you know it," Laura said, her voice coming out harsher than she meant it to be.

"You know why I have to go, Laura."

"It doesn't make sense to me, though."

"Well, it does to me," Cordell said quietly.

Laura lifted her chestnut head, the red-gold highlights shimmering under the lamps. "You just use that for an excuse, Ash."

"Laura!" Her father spoke sharply. "That's enough."

Mrs. Delsing broke the awkward moment of silence with her well-modulated tones: "We're going to miss you boys almost as if you were our own."

"We'll probably drift back in the fall," Tannehill drawled. "Time to help round up your beef."

"Where you headin' anyway?" demanded Fritz,

disregarding his father's frowning gesture. "You been just about everywhere already."

Ash Cordell smiled. "Not quite, son. We'll maybe hit west into the Madrelinos this trip. First off, anyway."

"If you stop in Trelhaven, you could look for that niece of ours," Mrs. Delsing suggested. "She calls herself Nita Dell, although her name is Delsing, the same as ours."

"It's just as well if Nita doesn't use our name," Laura said coldly. "You'll find her in the lowest honkytonk in town, I imagine."

"Now, Laura," protested her mother. "Nita is a wild one, but the poor girl never had much of a chance to be any different. She's the daughter of Dan's brother, and her folks were killed by Apaches when Nita was just a baby."

Laura winced and half raised a hand, her blue eyes flitting to Cordell's face, which had gone bleak and old like something carved in dark weathered stone. But her mother didn't know, couldn't be blamed, and Cordell was accustomed to suffering such unintentional thrusts in masked silence.

"They'll do well to stay away from Nita Dell, Mom," said Laura. "That girl means trouble for anybody who goes near her."

Mrs. Delsing shook her graying head. "I thought perhaps they could persuade the poor girl to come back here and live, Laura."

Dan Delsing interrupted his daughter's response with a large lifted hand. "I think maybe Laura is right in this case. Ranch life is too tame for Nita. She has chosen her course, and I'm afraid we'll have to let her go."

"All right, Dan. But I still think it's a shame."

"Who cares about that painted-up Nita?" cried Fritz. "You through, Ash? Come on out and do a little drawin' and shootin' with me and Tan."

"Ash and I are going for a walk, Fritz," said Laura.

"Who wants to go for a walk?" the boy asked in disgust. "Ash promised to tell me about that caper at Fort Washakie on the Wind River, up in northern Wyoming."

Cordell saluted and grinned at the youngster. "I'll tell you later, Fritz, or Tan can give you the story. Tan lies even better than I do, and he was really the big man in that jamboree. Comin' from him, it ought to be real good."

"Girls!" said Fritz, making an epithet of it.

"Have to make allowances for 'em, kid," smiled Cordell.

Fritz nodded his golden head. "Then they wonder why a man wants to get out and hit the open trail!"

Everyone laughed but the boy, and Laura said: "I'll be ready as soon as the dishes are done, Ash."

"You go along now, Laura," said Dan Delsing.

"I'll help Mom with the dishes. Be like old times, won't it, Mom?"

"See that you don't break as many as you used to," scolded Mom Delsing, to conceal how pleased she was by her husband's offer.

Chapter II

The brief twilight had deepened into dusk and then darkness, and it was full night as they strolled out along the irrigation ditch toward Bittersweet Creek. The air smelled cleanly of new grass and tender young leaves, spiced with sage, and the early stars sparkled in the night-blue northern sky above the lofty jagged peaks of the Shellerdines. A saber of a moon was rising over the Madrelino ramparts in the west, a golden blade tinged faintly red, and Cordell thought of how it would be up in that mountain wilderness.

He turned to look behind at the Big Barrancas, far beyond Hatchet in the east, dark, immutable and mysterious, massed high and blending into the star-flecked heavens. The secret to which he had been seeking the key all his life lay locked in one of those great mountain ranges. Cordell had hunted them all without finding it, but the search would go on as long as he lived. This was what kept him on the move, driving, nagging and tormenting him relentlessly. The memory of a certain valley in the mountains, where he had lived as a child. Cordell could never rest until he found that valley again, for he believed that in it was the clue to his identity, the fateful story of his family, the reason his father and mother had died violently there.

"It won't let you rest, will it, Ash?" the girl asked kindly.

"I reckon not," Cordell said. "It's always with me, Laura, awake or asleep, wherever I go."

"It's strange that nobody knows of such a valley."

"Strange?" He spoke through his teeth like a man in pain. "There are men who know, but they won't tell. I could make them talk, but I don't know who they are or where to find them."

"It's so hopeless, Ash," she murmured. "There's nothing to go on, not a trace or a thread. And it's wrecking your whole life, Ash."

"I can't help it, Laura. You don't understand what it's like not to know who you are, who your folks were, anythin' about yourself or your people. A man doesn't feel whole, Laura."

"There are lots of orphans in the world."

"Sure!" Cordell said fiercely. "But how many of them hear, and all but see, their parents murdered? How many of them never learn a single thing about their folks—who they were, what they did, where they came from, what kind of people they were? You don't know, Laura."

"I know, Ash—in part, at least." Her voice was reassuring, soothing, like the friendly pressure of her hand on his long muscular arm. "I feel for you, Ash, and I wish I could help. But it seems too bad to waste your life—and mine."

"We're young, Laura. We've got plenty of time."

"We don't get any younger though. The years go faster all the time, Ash, and you can't bring them back. The clock won't stand still while you hunt for that valley. And when you find it—if you ever do—what's there, Ash?"

"I don't know," Cordell said miserably. "Maybe nothin', but I've got to go on lookin'. I can't stop, Laura. It's stronger than myself, my feelin' for you, and everythin' else. Probably I'm a plain fool—surely I am—for not marryin' a girl like you. But I wouldn't be any good to you, Laura. I'd just ruin your life, too."

She smiled up at him. "I'm willing to risk that, Ash."

"No, I can't let you. You'd better cross me off, Laura, forget all about me."

"You're not asking much," Laura Delsing said. "Just the impossible. I'll never forget you, Ash. But perhaps I'll try to. I can't wait around forever."

Cordell gestured with his free hand clenched into a fist. "I'm not worth waitin' for anyway. I

27

haven't been too good, you know. At times I've done about anythin' I could to get away from that. Tried to drown it in whiskey, forget it in some woman's arms, lose it by fightin' with my bare hands or a gun. None of it did any good, Laura, but it shows you the kind of man I am."

"I know the kind of man you are," she said simply. "I guess I wouldn't want an angel or a saint, Ash. They'd be kind of out of place in a country like this Carikaree."

They walked in silence for an interval. The night grew more luminous as the moon climbed, paling from gold to silver in the starry sky. The Bittersweet was before them now, rippling with a silken swish among the white-frothed boulders, glinting dappled where the light fell through the frail-leaved branches of cottonwoods and willows. And there was the blackened burned-out ruin of the old Woodlee homestead, on a shelf over the stream. Cordell started to tell her what the Garriotts had done there, and about his good friend Bob Woodlee, but he stopped short, recalling that the Double-D lay in similar peril before the same Hatchet forces.

Those Garriotts sure had a lot to answer for, and Cordell meant to call them to account before he was finished. Old Gurney, the monarch; big handsome Gene; and the lank coyote-faced Kyler —they'd all pay before Cordell got through with them, and with blood.

"I'm worried about Hatchet," said Laura Delsing, as if reading his morbid thoughts, or perhaps it was the charred debris of the Woodlee place that prompted her words.

"Didn't Kyler offer you full protection once?" Cordell inquired, with some sarcasm and malice.

The girl's smile was wry. "Yes, but only in return for certain favors." It was her turn to be malicious. "Do you recommend that I accept, Ash?"

"Not exactly," he said grimly. "I'm goin' to have to kill that Kyler anyway, sooner or later. I've known it since we were kids. There's some decency in Gene, but none at all in Kyler. If he ever bothers you, Laura, that'll be all I need."

"He used to ride around quite often. Then you and Tan came, and Kyler stayed away." Laura sighed. "I suppose he'll start coming again when he hears that you've gone."

"Tell him to keep clear or I'll kill him," Cordell said with soft intensity. "If I have to shoot my way through every gunhand the Garriotts have got!"

"That won't be enough to scare Kyler off, Ash."

"Shoot him yourself, then."

"You want me to hang?" Laura asked, laughing hollowly. "You forget that Garriotts are not to be shot in this country, Ash."

"Their time'll come," Cordell said. "I'll see that it does."

They ceased walking and stood on the moonlit

river bank. Laura was rather tall for a woman, but her burnished chestnut head reached but a little above Cordell's rangy wide shoulder. The perfume of her hair came to him, and Cordell looked at her, something catching like a taut pain in his throat. She was lovely of face and figure, lithely graceful in either action or repose, slender but fully rounded and curved.

Gilded curls toppled, casual and charming, on her broad pure brow, and her eyes were wide and warmly bright, level and direct. There was an austere sculptured beauty about her high cheek-bones, the clean jaws and firm chin, the flawless line of her throat, but this was relieved by the slight tilt of her nose, made gracious by the generous width of her full-arched, handsome mouth. The nose was imperfect and human, pert and humorous, and the mouth had a rich earthy quality. In the two features that were not chiseled to perfection lay Laura Delsing's greatest attractiveness.

She was so breathtaking in the moonlight that it hurt Cordell to look at her, and with a pulsing ache in his throat he took her firmly and tenderly into his arms. For a moment she was still and unresponsive there, staring gravely up at the angular strong-boned bronze of his face. He has the strangest saddest gray eyes, she thought, eyes that actually change color. They could be a gay reckless blue, twinkling and devilish; or they could be a cold bitter green, full of menace and fury; or clear plain gray. And tonight there was white fire in their depths. Laura's arms went around his lean-muscled frame, and her mouth lifted warm and eager to meet his firm clean lips.

The long embrace left them breathless and deeply awed, looking at one another with solemn reverent wonder, shaken to the core. Cordell held her away at arm's length then, turning his high tawny head from side to side, as if he were stunned and bewildered. "No, Laura, no," he whispered softly.

"Yes, Ash," she whispered, with a woman's calm acceptance of what had to be. "It's there for us, Ash, real and right, honest and good, meant to be. It's ours, Ash, yours and mine. There'll never be anyone else for either of us. You know that, and I know it."

Cordell moaned faintly, low in his throat. "But I'm goin' away, Laura; I've got to go. This time I think I'll find it; I've got the feelin' it's close. I'll find it up in the Madrelinos, Laura, and then I'll come back—to you."

"No, you won't find it, Ash." She bowed her head slowly, the moonbeams touching the soft curls with pale fire. "And you won't always be coming back, Ash—to me or to anyone. There have been too many close ones, Ash, and a man's luck runs out after a while. It's now or never for us, Ash."

"I've got to go," Cordell said again, his voice flat and dull. "I can't give it up, Laura; there's somethin' inside that won't let me quit. But I'll always come back, Laura, and you've got to be waitin'."

Her bent head moved in vague negation. "I can't promise, Ash. Not anything, not any more. If you go, you go, that's all."

"I can't help goin'!" he said desperately, struggling helplessly for the power to convince her, make her comprehend.

She looked up at him in final appeal. "How do you know there's any such valley? You were so young then, Ash. How could you tell if you did come onto it? Places change in almost twenty years."

"I know it's somewhere in these mountains around the Carikaree. I can still see how it looked, Laura. Buttes and rivers and waterfalls don't change much. I'll know it when I get to it all right. It's there and I'll find it."

"Go ahead then, Ash," she said quietly. "I won't try to hold you. Maybe you will find it, after all. I'll be hoping for you, Ash, always. If that's what you want and need, then I want it, too."

They sat down on the grassy bank, Laura cradled in Cordell's left arm, her fragrant head pillowed on his shoulder. They were silent and thoughtful now, lulled by the smooth rustling murmur of the Bittersweet, breathing in the damp freshness of running water and green things budding and growing. A whippoorwill called its three distinct notes from a stand of cedar, and off in the distant foothills a coyote barked and a wolf bayed mournfully at the moon. The thin shrill clamor of frogs rose from a swampy section upstream, and fireflies traced erratic patterns in greenish-white streaks of light under the trees. The feeling of spring was everywhere about them, sap flowing beneath the bark, new life stirring in the earth, the air soft and mellow, moistly caressing their heads and faces.

Ash Cordell was back in that lost mountain valley of his childhood. He must have been about ten at the time, which would have made Clem around eight, and Sue Ellen six years old or so. The other two remembered little or nothing of those early days, and Ash's memories were mostly blurred, dim and distorted. But he recalled sharply certain physical features of the landscape, and a few small details about his father and mother.

It was high in the mountains, because the air was thin and keen, and some of the slopes rising around it were above the timberline, naked and barren in their steep thrust above the last stunted gnarled pines and twisted silvery aspens. A crescent-shaped valley, walled in by sharp talus slopes and sheer cliffs, watered by a sparkling cold stream that flowed roughly from south to north, the curved length of the depression. Willows and cottonwoods were scattered along the low shelving banks, and grass grew thick and tall on the valley floor, remarkable graze for such an elevation, his father had told him.

At the north end of the crescent, the river spilled thunderously over the rimrock in a two-hundred-foot waterfall, a roaring white-spumed cataract. In the constant dense clouds of mist that rose from the falls, rainbows might be seen whenever the sun struck right. Guarding this northern end of the valley, rearing in stark monstrous majesty over the waterfall, was the landmark that Cordell knew he would recognize instantly. A vast towering butte, which his mother had called the Cathedral, spired and steepled, arched and buttressed, like angular soaring Gothic architecture. Yes, he remembered the strange words his mother had used in describing it, how she had said: "God is the greatest of all architects, Ashburn." Cordell didn't know how or why he should recall those things, but they had always been with him. Perhaps because he had so few memories of his parents, he had striven to retain those.

The Cathedral caught the first long level rays of the rising sun each morning, and was touched first with crimson, then with gold. And every evening the sunset painted its myriad pinnacles, towers and arches in lavish and fantastic shades of every hue, transforming the great shattered mass of rock into a gorgeous magic castle, complete with turrets and bastions, ramps and parapets. *"A palace of splendor,"* his mother had said. *"Straight from fairyland."* It was her words about the butte that he remembered best about his mother. That and the clean lavender smell of her.

His father hadn't paid too much attention to the Cathedral, beyond giving it a casual tribute now and then, probably more to please Mother than anything else. His father had smoked pipes and been a hunter, smelling of tobacco, sunburned sweated leather and oiled steel, a masculine and not unpleasant aroma. A big man with a deep grave voice, silent much of the time and rather forbidding, but jolly and friendly when he joked and laughed. He hunted and shot mountain goats, elk and deer and bear, sometimes a lynx or bobcat. He trapped beaver, marten and mink along the streams lower down the mountainsides. Sometimes he took Ash hunting with him and showed him how to handle a gun.

"We aren't always going to live this way, Ash," his father had told him once. "It's only for a little while, son. We've got a place in the world, and we're going back to it before long. I won't have my children grow up like wild animals in this wilderness, and your mother wasn't meant for this kind of life either. But we've got to hang on here for a time, Ash boy."

Then one day his father had said they were

going to move back into civilization, such as it was out in this God-forsaken country. But *They* came, before the Cordell family could move. Ash always thought of them simply as "They." Some day he would learn who and where They were, and They would go down under his blasting guns.

Now Ash Cordell shuddered and stiffened rigid as the memory of that horror came screaming back in his mind, and Laura Delsing knew and understood his agony, pressing his big tense hand in both of hers.

The Cordells had lived in a log house near the center of the valley, and on this particular day Mother had suddenly hustled the three children through the hidden trapdoor into the cellar that Dad had dug for a storeroom. At the foot of the ladder she had clasped and kissed them each in turn, warning them to stay quietly down there until they were called up, and Ash had noticed that she was frightened and fighting to keep back the tears.

"What is it—Indians?" he'd asked. "If it is, let me come up; I can use a gun."

His mother had laughed a trifle hysterically. "No, it's not Indians. It may not be anything. You stay here, Ashburn, and take care of Clement and Sue Ellen. It won't be long." She had kissed him again, harder than ever before, differently somehow, and this time her cheeks had been streaming wet. Then she had hurried up the ladder, dropped the trapdoor in place, and covered it with the bearskin rug. The pure lavender fragrance of her lingered faintly in the sour musty dampness of the basement until the smell of raw earth and mold obscured it.

Left crouching there in the dank smothering darkness, Sue Ellen had begun to cry and Clem had started complaining, but Ash had finally scared them into shutting up. He had been brimming with terror, panic and despair himself, but he'd tried to act calm and brave as befitted the elder son of the house. It had come to him that his father and mother had been afraid ever since he could remember, afraid of somebody's coming. And now *They* were here. He had known then he would never see Mother and Dad alive again, and he had climbed the ladder with a terrible shrieking inside him, tearing and rending him apart.

Below Ash the other children commenced to sob again, but he was listening through the plank floor to the oncoming beat of hoofs, the creak of leather and jingle of bridles outside, and then the hoarse harsh voices and stomping boots overhead. He could sense the unleashed anger and hatred, the threat of violence and death in the trampled room above him, and once he heard his mother's voice go up in shrill protest, and break off with the sound of a vicious meaty impact, the sound of a hard open hand against a soft cheek. Ash writhed on the ladder, and his father's voice flared out raging, and then there was a quick rush of feet and the sound of another blow, this one more savage and solid.

"We sent them away," his mother had screamed defiantly. "You'll never find them, you murderous beasts!"

"They'll never know what happened," rumbled a strange voice. "They're too young to know anythin' anyhow." And there was laughter, jarring, mocking, the most hateful sound the boy had ever heard. "Let's get it done with," that same rough voice burred on, and gunshots blasted out, roaring and reverberating in the cabin, coming in swift succession.

Ash Cordell almost fell off the ladder then, retching with a horrible sickness, but he clung to the gritty rungs, set his teeth, and butted his young head up gently against the trapdoor. Carefully he inched it upward, nausea sweeping his ten-year-old body in waves, until he could peer through a slit under the shaggy edge of the bearskin and see a narrow portion of the floor. Just the floor and the dusty boots pacing to and fro, riders' boots with cruel-looking spurs clinking as they dragged.

The reek of gunpowder struck his nostrils and clogged his throat, and hot tears scalded his eyes dazzlingly as he choked back the vomit and kept his aching head steady under the heavy pressure of the wooden trap. He wanted to bust up there and fight them all, a kid of ten and barehanded against their guns, and he might have done it if it hadn't been for his little brother and sister wailing pitifully in the nether gloom. Silently, the words flaming over and over in his brain, he was cursing the killers, cursing them and swearing to get them when he grew up. And straining to see some identifying sign or mark on them. Nothing but boots, swinging swaggering boots with long-shanked large-roweled spurs tinkling softly on the planks.

Then there was one boot in particular, heavy, misshapen and dragging grotesquely, with a thick built-up sole and heel, the monstrous boot of a cripple. That was something to look for, something to search the world over for, if he had to. Ash let the sight of that deformed boot sear itself into his mind.

The men were getting ready to leave now, and the smell of coal oil came strongly to the boy, followed by the crackle of fire and the odor of burning wood. Ash wanted to get a glimpse of the murderers, but he had to think about getting Sue Ellen and Clem out of there; soaked in kerosene, the house would blaze up like a torch.

Flinging the trapdoor open, bearskin and all, Ash saw the lifeless riddled bodies in a far corner, his mother and father lying dead in their blood, and a tremendous fury boiled up in him like madness. He looked out a window and saw the riders, far down the valley toward the southern pass, turn in their saddles to glance back at the burning cabin. They were too far away to recognize or shoot at, but he knew one of them was a cripple, and sometime he would see that evil-looking boot again.

While the flames roared hungrily about the walls, Ash ducked back into the tomblike blackness of the cellar to haul Sue Ellen and Clement up the ladder and out the back door of the blazing structure. There was nothing he could do for his father and mother; the fire was already leaping high about them, and they were beyond further hurt.

Sprawled a safe distance away from the heat and acrid smoke of the conflagration, the three children rested on the earth and watched the only home they knew burn down into a charred black framework of desolate ruin, a funeral pyre for their parents.

The next day an old prospector found them on a down-mountain trail, and took them into the nearest homestead in the Carikaree Valley. From there they were transported by various conveyances to the town of Cadmus, and shortly thereafter Gurney Garriott took them home with him to Hatchet. . . .

Laura Delsing's voice startled him back to present reality: "Don't torture yourself so, Ash; please don't. It's time to walk back anyway. I'll get you a big drink of Dad's whiskey."

Cordell smiled somberly at her. "Not much company for a girl, am I? Sorry, Laura."

"It's all right, Ash. Being with you is enough for me."

Cordell leaned over and pressed his mouth against the sweet fullness of hers, finding as much peace and pleasure there as he would ever know —until he found Cathedral Valley and the truth about his family and himself, and the men who had murdered his mother and father some seventeen years before.

Walking back toward Double-D with his arm around the girl's firm shoulders, Cordell thought he and Tannehill had better take off tomorrow. It was going to be hard to leave Laura and her family, but hanging around wouldn't make it any easier.

Ash Cordell had to go, and keep on going, until he discovered what he was seeking, or went down somewhere along the way. There was always the chance of that in this country, particularly for a man who had used his fists and guns as much as Cordell had.

Chapter III

Two mornings later they rode out of Delsing's Double-D, Cordell on his rawboned slate-colored roan, Tannehill on his big gray-mottled buckskin, both men tall and easy in the saddle, not looking back once their farewells were made. They headed west, the early sun still red and soaring clear of the Big Barrancas 'behind them, its flat rays laying elongated shadows on the broad sweep of Wagon Mound.

They traveled without talking much; there was no need of words between them after all they had shared and experienced in far-flung frontier places. They had been riding together for seven years now, through all the Western territories from Texas to the Dakotas, trail-driving cattle, working ranches, freighting and mining, gambling, drinking and fighting. And always hunting for that lost valley, or someone who knew of it and the Cordell family.

Seven years back Ash Cordell had been twenty, two years away from Hatchet and cutting it on his own, wild, tough and reckless as they came, even in a country that bred so many with those qualities. In a Dodge City saloon, Cordell had called a house man for dealing off the bottom, gun-whipping the gambler down when he tried to draw. The owner and his strong-arm boys were about to gang up on Cordell when Tannehill threw into the game on Cord's side. The fighting became general and chaotically confused: riders and townsmen against the saloon employees. It ended with the place a shambles, unconscious and dead bodies strewn amidst the wreckage, and Cordell and Tannehill had stumbled out of it together, tattered and bleeding, carrying bottles salvaged from the ruined bar. They had been together ever since.

Tannehill was about the same age as Cordell, twenty-seven now, as tall as Cord's six-foot height but built sparer and slighter, slender and sinewy. Tannehill was rawhide-tough and whip-limber, with an amazing amount of explosive power packed into his lean, long-limbed frame. His voice and actions were lazy, indolent, but he could move like lightning when he had to. Tannehill's brown hair had a rust-red tinge, and his mild brown eyes held a yellowish glint when he was aroused. His face was lean to gauntness, weathered to the tan of cordovan leather, cheekbones, nose and jawbones standing out sharply. He smiled easily and often, a friendly boyish smile that made him look like a kid of nineteen or younger. Men said that Tannehill would have followed Cordell into the bottom-most pit of Hades, barefooted and empty-handed, against all the legions of Satan.

If Tan had ever heard this, he would probably have grinned and drawled: "Why, sure, I reckon. If I figured there was a drink down there."

They splashed across the shallows of Bittersweet Creek, speaking of Bob Woodlee as they viewed the rubbled remnants of the Woodlee ranch, and went on to drop from the western rim of Wagon Mound. On their right towered the Shellerdines, tier on serrated tier of stark grandeur, and on their left the Bittersweet curled across the greening bronze lowlands toward the Carikaree and Cadmus Flats. Ahead was the gray bulk of Confederate Ridge, and they pointed for that.

Cordell was thinking that he should have swung southward and followed the Bittersweet down to Cadmus, where Sue Ellen and Clement were living with Ma Muller in her Hillhouse Hotel, since Ash had removed them from Hatchet and arranged for their new home. Sue Ellen waited on tables, and Clem worked as desk clerk and handy man. It was an ideal setup, because Ma Muller couldn't have been any fonder of her own flesh and blood than she was of the Cordells. Yes, he ought to go in and see how the kids were getting along. They were pretty well grown up now, and Ma Muller couldn't always handle them the way she used to.

There were times when Clem fretted irritably against his routine tasks and humdrum existence in the hotel, envying Ash the unrestricted freedom and the excitement of his roving life. Ash would have taken him out on the trail occasionally but for the fact that Clem lacked the necessary toughness, sharpness and self-assurance. At least it seemed to Ash that he did. Clem had never taken to horses, guns and fighting the way Ash did. Clem was quieter, gentler, kinder—and softer. A well bred carriage horse, while Ash was a wild stallion. Clem was twenty-five now, but to Ash he was still a small kid brother to be protected and sheltered.

And Sue Ellen was a young lady of twenty-three, a very pretty young lady, blonde and gray-eyed, her hair much lighter than Ash's, golden where his was a dusky bronze, her features delicate and refined, yet stamped with character and a proud willful strength. It was difficult to realize that his little sister had become a woman, fully matured in mind and body, and it struck Ash with a cold shock that she would be getting married one of these days. The idea was unpleasant to him. There weren't any men good enough for Sue Ellen. Tannehill was, of course, but Sue Ellen regarded him as another older brother in the family.

She'd probably fall for some no-good stuffed-shirt in town, with long pomaded hair and a store suit, whose very presence would set Ash's teeth on edge and make his knuckles itch yearningly.

Big Gene Garriott, the good-looking Garriott boy, had tried to court Sue Ellen when they were all kids together on Hatchet, and even after the Cordells moved into the hotel in Cadmus Flats, but repeated beatings and threats of death from Ashburn had finally discouraged Gene. It was funny, mused Ash: in early boyhood at the ranch Gene had always licked Ash, but in later years it was Ash who administered the thrashings. It had never been easy either way, however, for they were evenly matched, Ash's superior speed compensating for his lack of bulk. Gene was a strapping giant, like old Gurney, his father.

Well, if Sue Ellen's choice of a husband was too bad, Ash would just naturally break up the wedding, that was all. He shook his head, swearing softly and spitting aside. Tannehill edged his buckskin over and held out a plug of tobacco. "You're spittin' kinda dry, Cord." Grinning and accepting the plug, Cordell bit off a generous jawful. Chewing was a comfort on the gusty open trail, where the rolling and lighting of cigarettes was impractical.

That afternoon they skirted the southern flank of Confederate Ridge, lining on toward Sulphur Springs where they planned to camp the first night, the sun in their faces as it slid slowly down the molten blue sky toward the high-ranked Madrelino crests.

"Tomorrow night we'll make Trelhaven,"

drawled Tannehill. "It'll seem kind of nice to hit a real town again."

"We'll load up with supplies there," Cordell said, "and head for the highlands."

"We better load up with liquor too. It's been a long time since I drank my fill, Cord. Let's lay over an extra day or so, to get drunk and taper it off."

"Sure, Tan; it might do us good to howl a little. Reckon you'll be lookin' up that Nita Dell girl too, won't you?"

"I might, at that," grinned Tannehill. "Like I said about liquor, it's been a long empty stretch."

"Maybe we'll run across Bob Woodlee," said Cordell. "Last I heard he was freightin' out of Trelhaven."

Tannehill nodded in pleasurable anticipation. "Sure like to see Woody again. If he's the boy he used to be, Woody'll help us celebrate some."

"A rider from Chimney Rocks was tellin' me Woody had himself a girl now, a real bad case of love."

"May it be a false and idle rumor," Tannehill said. "Anythin' like that cramps a man's style somethin' awful, when it comes to hoorawin' around paintin' up a town."

They rode on into the lowering sun, loose and lounging in their double-rigged saddles, flat-crowned wide-brimmed hats slanted against the afternoon glare. Rawhide riatas were tied fast to their horns, Texas style, and behind the cantles were slicker-wrapped bedrolls, a buckskin jacket tied to Cordell's, a blue jumper on Tannehill's. They wore checkered shirts, bright scarfs, leather vests with convenient pockets, and snug-legged pants tucked into handmade hickory-peg boots. The spurs were ornamental, but the Colt .44's in the low tied-down sheaths were not. Canteens jogged at the pommels, and carbine butts protruded from saddle scabbards.

Their clothes and equipment were conventional, but some indefinable quality in the men themselves made them stand out in the eyes of the people in lonely ranches and homesteads who witnessed their passing. Something in their rangy height and keen tanned profiles, the set of their heads and shoulders, an effortless ease of manner and motion. Two more drifting cowhands, but with a difference. These men were looking for something more than another job or a night in town or a painted woman. These two had done a lot of dangerous living high and hard with guns in hand and death before them. It left its brand on such men, elusive but unmistakable.

They had fought and killed, from necessity perhaps, and they would fight and kill again when the occasion called for it. Men like that were a hundred to one to die with their boots on and guns smoking in their hands. "There'll be a shootin' scrape in Trelhaven or somewhere," the watching people said. "And them two hard-cases'll be dead in the street, or on the run for the high country."

As they rocked on into the reddening blaze of the sun, Tannehill remarked: "You ever think of givin' it up, Cord? Sometimes I wonder. Sometimes, they say, it's better to let dead things lay dead."

"I know, Tanny. I've thought it out from every angle there is, I guess. But it isn't in me to give it up." Cordell softened his tone. "If you're gettin' tired of it, Tan . . ."

"Heck, I got nothin' better to do, Cord!" said Tannehill. "It's you I'm thinkin' about. You and maybe—Laura."

"It's rough on her, all right. I tried to tell her, Tan. I wouldn't keep any strings on her."

Tannehill smiled soberly. "You don't have to, that's the trouble. She's for you, Cord, no matter what."

"And I'm for her, Tan. We'll be goin' back to Wagon Mound. But first, there's a place in the Madrelinos an old mountain man told me about. He wasn't much on words, but it sounded somethin' like it."

"It beats me, Cord. All the places and the folks we've seen, and nary a lead to that valley. Never a word on your family. Nobody that ever heard of them. Or if they do know anythin', they're afraid to let it out. You ever figure the Garriotts in on it some way?"

"Considerable," said Ash Cordell. "They aren't given to helpin' strangers, as a rule, like they helped us. It isn't like old Gurney to give anythin' away for free. I thought maybe it was his conscience, as if that old buzzard had one! But I never got anywhere along that line, Tan. Not a single sign or hint on Hatchet."

"People think it's a mite odd and unnatural, your hatin' the Garriotts, after Gurney took you in and raised you."

"It most likely is, Tan. But I can't help that any more than I can help breathin'. It's that natural, in my blood and my bones. You think it's unnatural, Tan?"

"Heck, no!" laughed Tannehill. "I hate 'em myself, without any real personal reason. I'm hopin' they'll leave the Delsings alone."

"By grab, they'd better!" Cordell said, quietly intense, the muscles ridged along his strong jaws, his eyes burning green and cold.

"We never did find one of them built-up cripple-footed boots, did we?" Tannehill sought to change the subject. "You got me so I always look a man's boots over pretty sharp, Cord."

"We'll see one some day. Sulphur Springs ahead, Tan."

Tannehill sighed and stretched in the leather. "I wish it was Trelhaven. After workin' eight months without hardly a break, I feel like a big bad curly wolf from the high timber. I got to howl before long, Cord, else I'll bust wide open!"

"We'll do some howlin' tomorrow night, son," Cordell said with a bleak smile. "There's a little pressure built up in me likewise."

Chapter IV

Ash Cordell woke up groaning. He was lying fully dressed on a bed in a room he did not recognize immediately. A large room with another bed in it, unoccupied at present. It was daylight—the rays from the windows stabbed painfully at his glazed eyeballs—but he had no conception of the time. His tongue was swollen too large for his parched mouth, stiff with a poisonous crust, and his throat was on fire. He placed the room now in the Elkhorn Hotel in Trelhaven. They had checked in last evening, or was it two nights ago? He wondered what had become of Tannehill.

Pain rocketed through his skull as Cordell pushed himself into a sitting position and dropped his numb legs heavily over the edge of the bed. There were bottles all over the place, and he stared blankly at them, shook his throbbing head and groaned again. Water, he had to have water. Rising with an effort, he shuffled woodenly to the table, where a white pitcher stood among the dark whiskey bottles. There was water in it, lukewarm but wet, and Cordell gulped greedily at it, spilling some down his chest.

The water loosened the evil stiffness of his tongue, eased the taut burning of his throat, and Cordell felt better. Tramping up and down the floor, he flexed and swung his arms, limbered and kicked out with his legs, gratified as the blood and life began flowing once more in his body. A glance out the window told him it was late afternoon. He went on moving around, exercising, until his head cleared and his muscles were responding, working smoothly again.

Cordell found a bottle with some liquor in it, and took a good drink to cut the vile taste in his mouth. He washed his hands and face, soaked his head, toweled briskly, and combed his sandy, sun-streaked brown hair. Feeling immeasurably refreshed, he had another drink, shaped a cigarette, and sat down in a chair by the window. He was all right now, or nearly so. It was wonderful to be young, in fine health and condition, able to recover so rapidly.

The hectic blur of the past twenty-odd hours came into focus as he smoked. They had arrived about sundown, stabled the horses, had a few drinks, enjoyed the luxury of barbershop baths and shaves and haircuts. Then supper, a little polite drinking in saloons, and a lot of plain and fancy drinking in this hotel room. Bob Woodlee was out of town, so they hadn't seen him, but they had met a lot of people in the gambling houses, barrooms and dance halls of Trelhaven. Yes, they had even met Nita Dell, the runaway cousin of Laura and Fritz Delsing. Someone had warned them that she was Kyler Garriott's girl, and somebody else inferred that Bob Woodlee was sweet on her. Nita was quite a number, and she'd never belong to any one man, Cordell was certain of that.

Putting on his hat and strapping on his gun-belt, Cordell was about to go in search of Tannehill when he heard him coming along the corridor, his voice raised in rollicking song. The door opened, and Ash saw that Nita Dell was with him, dark and vivid with impish black eyes, pouting provocative scarlet lips, and a generously curved figure. She wore a gown of red satin that flared widely toward the floor.

"See what I found, Cord," said Tannehill. "Ain't she pretty? Ain't she cuter'n a speckled hound pup, though?"

Nita Dell swayed close to Cordell, her sensuous face lifted, dark eyes flirting up at him. "I like you," she said childishly, and he saw that she was drunk. "You're big and strong, and ugly and beautiful."

"Hey, what's the matter with me, Nita?" demanded Tannehill. "You think I ain't big and strong and beautiful? Listen, where I come from the women just claw each other's eyes out over me, gal."

Nita Dell laughed. "Go back where you come from, Tanny boy." She moved even closer to Cordell, so that her perfume filled his nostrils. Suddenly her arms snaked about him with surprising strength and she stood holding him closely, pressing and swaying as if to slow music. It was because he had refused to dance with her last night, Cordell knew. Smiling faintly, he disengaged her arms and thrust her gently away.

"Better get her out of here, Tan."

"But why? We just got here, Cord."

"She's drunk, for one thing."

Tannehill laughed uproariously. "So am I, and so was you."

"She's Kyler Garriott's girl, for another."

"Kyler's not here, Kyler's in Cadmus," Nita chanted. "Don't be afraid of Kyler."

"What about Bob Woodlee?" asked Cordell.

Nita Dell laughed contemptuously. "Him? Why, he just loves me to death. He wants to marry me!" She laughed as if at some huge ludicrous joke.

Cordell's broad mouth straightened thinly, and his angular face froze hard. "I'm goin' for a walk, Tan."

"Have a drink here with us, Cord. We're just stayin' for one drink."

"See you downstairs," Cordell said, and heard

54

the girl spitting foul curses after him as he shut the door from the outside. Some wildcat, this relative of the Delsings. If what she said was true, he felt very sorry for Bob Woodlee.

At the head of the stairway leading down into the lobby, something compelled Cordell to halt and turn back, some primitive sense of lurking danger behind him. The corridor was vacant when he peered around the corner, but even as he watched a door opened across the hall from their room. Two men appeared, vaguely familiar in the shadowy dimness of the hallway, and paused before the room which Cordell had just left. Loosening his gun in its holster, Cordell paced back down the long gloomy corridor toward them, treading lightly, eyes alert and right hand spread-fingered for the draw. They were Hatchet men, as Cordell had suspected, the squat blocky Skowron and the lithe handsome Thorner.

"Lookin' for somebody, boys?" inquired Cordell.

Tonk Thorner, the nearest, whirled to face Cordell, motioning Skowron back. "A pleasure, Cord, and sooner than I expected," Thorner said, debonair as ever and play-acting a bit. "You boys ought to know better than to play around Hatchet property."

"I didn't read any brand on it," Cordell said.

"It's there, Cord. And you was warned last night."

"So what'll it be, Tonk?"

Skowron's bloated face scowled under the stress of the moment, his small eyes blinking furiously. "One woman ain't enough for you, mister? The Delsing girl ain't enough, you got to go after Kyler's woman? That Delsing girl was Kyler's, till you hit Wagon Mound."

"Shut up, Skow," said Thorner. "This one is mine. You can have the drunk in there."

"So you want war?" Cordell said easily. "Too bad to start shootin' over a dance hall girl, Tonk."

"Whatever she is, she's Kyler Garriott's. Some people figure you been livin' a lot too long, Cordell, and I'm one of 'em. I been wantin' to get you in front of me for quite some spell." Tonk Thorner stood smiling, his elbows out wide, a poised and somewhat theatrical figure in the drab murky corridor.

"Well, you've got me," murmured Cordell. "Make your play."

Tonk Thorner swept into a two-handed draw, for which he was justly famous. Cordell's big right hand dipped and came up with fluid speed, thumbing off a shot as Thorner's guns cleared leather. The blast of Cordell's .44 lighted the hallway, the Colt kicking up hard in his hand, the report deafening between the walls. Thorner swiveled halfway around and bent in the middle, gutshot, his guns exploding into the floor with a thunderous sound. Pitching forward on his face, Tonk Thorner squirmed briefly, went rigid, then slumped slack and motionless.

Skowron exhaled raspingly and reached for his holster, half hidden behind Thorner until Tonk went down, and Cordell was switching his gun onto the second Hatchet man when the door slammed open and Tannehill came out behind a flaming gun barrel that bucked up, leveled, and lashed out with another bright roar. The short bulky Skowron jerked back under the walloping .44 slugs, fired ceilingward as he bounced brokenly off the wall, turned in a sagging lumbering circle, and landed flat on his back, crosswise of the corridor behind Thorner's silver-inlaid boots.

"That darn girl—tried to wrassle me down," panted Tannehill, as they crouched over the two fallen forms.

Nita Dell emerged wild-eyed from the room, and fled sobbing along the smoky hall, leaving a trail of perfume through the gunpowder.

"Looks like they planted her," Cordell said. "Had us all framed up, only it backfired on 'em." He completed his hasty examination. "Both still alive but not much chance for Thorner here. Skowron maybe'll pull through."

"The devil to pay, huh?" muttered Tannehill. "Wish I'd sobered up more. Reckon they'll hold us, Cord?"

"Not for long, Tan. They know us, they know Hatchet, and they know Nita Dell. The Garriotts aren't so popular in this west end of the Carikaree.

57

It was self-defense, their guns were fired, and the law here's got no use for Hatchet gunhands."

"But it'll be war with Hatchet from here on. We'll have all the Garriotts on our necks."

"Yes, we'll have that all right," agreed Ash Cordell.

Tannehill grinned boyishly. "Well, we can take care of 'em, Cord. If they don't come in too big a bunch. I'm goin' to sneak me a drink before the crowd gathers."

Heavy boots were clomping up the front stairs and rushing toward the corridor. "Not a bad idea, Tan," said Cordell, following him into the room. "And another good one is to get some of these bottles out of sight."

Three mornings later, they were cleared, free, and getting ready for their trek into the Madrelino Mountains.

Tonk Thorner was dead, but Skowron had a chance of recovery. Nita Dell had vanished, and Bob Woodlee hadn't returned as yet.

Cordell and Tannehill were buying provisions in a store when a queer prickle at the back of Cord's neck brought him around from the counter, and Tan turned with him. Bob Woodlee *had* come back. He was standing there staring narrowly at them, no greeting on his taut lips, no friendliness in his slitted eyes. His usually pleasant face was drawn and haggard, pale and sick-looking under the brown. The skirt of his cord coat was pulled back behind the gun-handle on his right hip. They said, "Howdy, Woody," in their old manner of greeting him, but Bob disregarded it and went on eyeing them with mixed pain and hatred.

"I heard all about it," Bob Woodlee said at last.

"Yeah, it was quite a ruckus," drawled Tannehill, trying to maintain the friendly smile that was beginning to make him feel foolish.

"Yes, it was. You ought to be real proud!"

Cordell leaned back on the counter, chewing his last piece of dried apricot. "What is this, Woody? You haven't gone over to Hatchet, have you?"

"Save your funny stuff, Cord. You know what it is. You had Nita Dell up in your hotel room, didn't you?"

"Sure, for a drink. She was sent up by Hatchet, so Thorner and Skowron would have an excuse to jump us."

"That's a lie!" Bob Woodlee said. "Hatchet's nothin' to her. Nita's all through with Kyler Garriott. She was *my* girl, Cord!"

"Well, we didn't know that, Woody."

"You know it now, and you're goin' to answer for it!"

"All we did was talk anyway," said Cordell.

"Look, Woody," interposed Tannehill. "I was the one that brought her to the room, boy. She was drunk when I met her, if you want it straight."

Woodlee glared at him. "I'll get to you too, Tan."

"Don't be a fool, Woody," said Tannehill disgustedly.

Cordell raised his hand. "We've been friends a long time, Woody."

"That's what hurts," Woodlee gritted. "That's what makes it so bad. I never thought I'd lift a gun against you, Cord, but I'm goin' to."

"Please, boys, please," muttered the distraught storekeeper. "Take your argument outside." Nobody paid the slightest attention to him, and he retreated with his quavering clerk.

"Don't do anythin' rash, Woody," said Cordell, earnest and pleading. "Us three been through a lot of times together."

Woodlee's laugh was dry, brittle. "Before it starts, I've got some news for you, Cord. You'd better get back to Cadmus Flats."

"What for?"

"A couple of things, Cord. Your sister's runnin' wild with Gene Garriott, they tell me. And your brother's hangin' around the girls in the Rio Belle every night!" There was a triumphant note in Woodlee's voice.

"You wouldn't lie, Woody—about that?" Cordell asked slowly.

"It's the truth. I just came from Cadmus."

Cordell glanced at Tannehill. "Maybe we better hit east instead of west, Tan."

"Anythin' you say, Cord."

Bob Woodlee motioned angrily. "First you got me to settle with."

"Woody, I've got no time for this foolishness," Cordell said wearily. "Go find your girl; nobody else wants her."

"You wanted her! She left a note for me, told me all about it."

"She's workin' for Hatchet, tryin' to get me killed. Can't you see that?" Cordell shook his head hopelessly. "Lay off, Woody. I don't want to have to draw on you."

"You're goin' to have to—or die without drawin'!" Woodlee grated, his face transfigured with emotion, his eyes fanatical. "Reach for it, Cord!"

Cordell straightened off the worn wood with a sigh, and looked over Woodlee's shoulder toward the front door, letting his eyes widen as he said: "We better wait and see what the sheriff wants."

Bob Woodlee barely turned his head, snapping it quickly back to the front and clawing at his gun, but Cordell was already lunging into him, legs driving hard, lifting and throwing Woodlee backward, smashing him down and grinding him into the plank floor. Woodlee's gun was half drawn, but Cordell had that right wrist clamped in a clutch of steel.

Fighting like a maniac, heaving, bucking and thrashing about in fury, Woodlee strove to break away, but Cordell was too strong and heavy on top of him, too swift and sure-handed. Powerless and sobbing for breath under the bigger man, Woodlee subsided at last, and Cordell tore the gun out of his numbed grasp and slid it along the boards to Tannehill.

"You ought to belt some brains into him, Cord," advised Tannehill, scooping up the gun and thrusting it under his waistband.

Cordell shook his head, climbed carefully off the other man, and stepped clear. Woodlee got up slowly, panting hard, and then hurled himself forward, swinging like a madman at Cordell's face and head. Ash ducked into a crouch and crowded in to grapple him, but Woodlee flung him off with an insane burst of strength and went on flailing away, landing now and then with jarring force.

Jolted, hurt, and stung to anger for the first time, Cordell went into a weaving fighting crouch and started using his own fists. Driving in, he beat Woodlee's arms down, battered him back half-way across the counter. When Woodlee came scrambling off it and onto his feet again, Cordell caught him with a left, straightening him up stiff and tall. Shifting and striding forward, Cordell struck with his right, a solid smash that sounded like a cleaver on the meat-block. Woodlee's head bobbed, twisting backward as his boots left the floor. He lighted on the back of his neck and shoulders at the base of the counter, his boots thudding down seconds later, his legs loosely asprawl and his body limp and senseless.

Ash Cordell, breathing hard and rubbing his knuckles, stood looking down at the unconscious bleeding man, regret and sorrow on his own bruised face. He beckoned the storekeeper. "We won't be needin' all that grub we ordered. We'll just take what we got in the saddlebags here, if you'll figure it up."

The man did so, between frightened furtive glances at the figure on the floor, and Cordell paid him, saying: "He'll be all right. Too bad it had to happen, and in your place. I want to get out before Woody comes to."

Tannehill was pacing back and forth, shaking his rusty brown head in disgust. "Over a good-for-nothin' little honkytonk girl that isn't worth the price of a drink. Which gives me a powerful thirst all at once, Cord."

"We've got plenty for the road, Tan. I don't want any more trouble with Woody." Cordell looked at the store man. "You'll take care of him?"

"Sure, sure, I know Bob. Never saw him act that way before, though. I'll bring him around."

"Here's his gun." Tannehill laid it on the smooth-worn wood. "Keep it out of sight a while and don't bring him around too quick."

"No sir, there's been enough shootin' here." The proprietor mopped his pale face with a purple handkerchief. "Not puttin' any blame on you two gentlemen, of course."

Tannehill eyed him severely. "This is a tough town. Two peace-lovin' pilgrims drift in real innocent, and everybody starts slingin' guns on 'em."

"Come on, Tanny," said Cordell, and they went out carrying their bulging saddlebags.

The storekeeper watched them go with a sigh of relief. "Tough town, peaceful pilgrims," he mumbled. "Seems to me all our trouble comes from Cadmus and the east end of the valley. Thought sure we was goin' to have another killin', and be buryin' young Bob Woodlee tomorrow. Fetch a bucket of water, Johnny, while I see if this boy's neck is broke."

They sold the pack-horse back to the livery barn owner, at a loss, and rode out of Trelhaven in a westerly direction. Well away from the town, they made a wide southward swing and circled back toward the east, threading through the stone columns of the Needles and crossing the rim of the Kiowa Desert.

Back in the Carikaree Valley they made camp for the night, talking late beside the friendly orange glow of the fire, smoking cigarettes and passing a bottle back and forth at long regular intervals. Ash Cordell was gravely worried by what Woodlee had told him about Sue Ellen and Clement. Since the Cordells were like his own family, Tannehill was likewise perturbed.

"It looks like a real shootin' war is buildin' up, Cord," drawled Tannehill.

"It had to come sometime, Tan. I always knew I'd have it out with the Garriotts some day, and I reckon the day has come." Cordell turned his head from side to side, his strong-boned face more angular than ever in the dull red glare of the slow flames, his hair like polished bronze in the firelight. "Everything's breakin' bad, Tan. It bothers me, Bob Woodlee comin' at us like that."

Tannehill nodded, the coppery highlights glinting across his head. "It leaves a bad taste, Cord, and a sick feelin' in the stomach. That's what the wrong kind of woman can do to a good man."

"Those kids, Sue Ellen and Clem," mused Ash Cordell. "I've had to look out for them ever since —well, I'll always have to. They don't belong in a country like this, Tan. It's all right for a bronco like me, but it's no good for them."

"We'll take care of 'em, pardner," Tannehill said softly.

In the morning, they struck the main highway along the Carikaree River and rode eastward into the rising red sun. Cordell had the feeling that he would never find his mountain valley now, that fate was against his seeing it again. He would live out his life here in the lowlands, defending his sister and brother and the Delsings against the overwhelming forces of Hatchet. With the odds as they were, it was apt to be a very short life.

Chapter V

Hillhouse Hotel stood on a low shelf of land overlooking the western end of Cadmus Flats, a large rambling structure with a double-galleried facade that commanded the length of Front Street, the main thoroughfare of the settlement. Ugly as it was, the old hotel had a certain dignity and character that, along with its reputation for comfort and cleanliness, plus the famed quality of Ma Muller's cooking, made it well known and popular throughout the region. The large bulk and aloof position of Hillhouse, over the head of the principal business street, set it apart from the commonplace huddle of the frame and adobe buildings on the flats below.

Tonight the supper hour was long past and the dining room closed, the place quiet and somnolent, with a few scattered groups of guests smoking and chatting in the lobby or on the front veranda. The dishes were done, the help gone for the evening, and Ma Muller was alone in the kitchen scrubbing absent-mindedly at an already shining clean tabletop.

She was troubled about Sue Ellen and Clem Cordell. She wished Ash would come home, yet she somehow dreaded his coming. Ash would be in a killing mood the moment he learned that Sue Ellen was keeping steady company with Gene Garriott, and it wasn't going to please Ash much more to find Clement fooling around with those girls in the Rio Belle. Well, they've got to grow up sometime, thought Ma Muller. They aren't kids any more, and Ash can't always live their lives for them. Ash isn't much older than they are, but he feels and acts like a father toward them. Maybe Ash has held them down too much, pampered and coddled them too long.

Hearing the slow clop of hoofs outside in the road leading back to the stable, Ma Muller moved to a window. "No more meal tonight, by the old Harry," she said firmly. "I don't care who it is, they'll get nothin' to eat here!" Her worn lined face was set harshly as she pressed it to the darkened glass, but it relaxed at once as she spotted the shadowy silhouettes of the two passing riders. Her faded blue eyes and tired features lighted up wonderfully with her smile.

"That boy knows somethin's wrong," she told herself, turning instinctively to a mirror on the wall. "He can smell trouble from one end of the Carikaree to the other." Dabbing at her wiry gray hair with veined, work-gnarled hands, she suddenly realized what she was doing and smiled cynically at her reflection. "Why, you poor old fool, you!" she murmured with a grimace.

"Primpin' like a silly schoolgirl with her first beau." Laughing in self-ridicule, she went to a cupboard and got out a bottle of whiskey and two glasses. Ma wouldn't have a barroom in her hotel, but she always kept something on hand for particular friends of hers, as well as for medicinal purposes.

Ma Muller was a large capable woman who carried her years lightly and well. She was still straight and sturdy in her clean gingham, strong-limbed and deep-bosomed, active and quick-moving. Her gray head was erect, calm and proud, her washed-blue eyes level and direct with pleasant wrinkles at the corners, her rather bold features dulled but little by time, trouble, and the disappointments of life.

When Ma Muller heard their boots on the back steps, she threw open the door and made her voice harsh and scornful. "Nothin' here for you saddle-tramps! Get along down to the Longhorn and the Rio Belle where you belong!"

"Listen to the woman talk," laughed Ash Cordell, coming forward into the mellow lamp-light and tossing his hat aside. He looked bigger and broader in the shoulders than ever, she thought: rawboned and rugged but moving with that easy fluid grace. Tough, with that brassy beard stubble glinting on his lean jaws, but hand-some too, his fine head gleaming blond in the light, his eyes dancing gray-blue, that charming smile changing him from a somber-faced man to a merry boy.

Then she was in those long powerful arms and laughing hard to keep the tears back, holding him tight and burying her face in his wide shoulder. Ash Cordell held her tenderly, stroking her silvery head with one big brown hand. "How are you, Ma? How've you been, Ma?"

"What do you care, you wanderin' renegade?" Ma Muller pushed away from him, and extended her hand to Tannehill. "Hullo, Tan, and welcome home. I can probably thank you again for gettin' *him* back here in one piece."

"Not me, Ma, not this trip," Tannehill grinned. "Cord kinda pulled me out of one this time."

Cordell sighted the bottle, and made for it with a gay shout of laughter. "Ma, you're still hittin' this stuff!" he accused her with mock severity. "It ain't becomin' to a woman, Ma, as I've told you before."

Ma Muller snorted. "It ain't becomin' to a man either, but you always got your nose in a glass!" She smiled then, beaming all over her face. "Set right down to it, boys. I'm happy to have you home. I'll fry you up a nice steak. You probably haven't had a real square meal since you left Hillhouse. Wash up over there, if you haven't got out of the habit. Here's a pair of towels for you." She got busy again over the stove she had so recently cleaned up for the night, while they scrubbed their hands and faces.

Back at the table they sat down with the bottle and drank a couple of quick toasts to Ma Muller. "Where are the kids, Ma?" inquired Cordell.

"Kids? No kids here, Ash. Oh, you mean Sue Ellen and Clem? They're around somewhere. I can't keep 'em on a leash, you know."

"Is Clem gettin' kinda wild, Ma?"

"Well, he's your brother, Ash. But I doubt if he'll ever be as skyhootin' wild and bad as you. He is takin' some interest in girls now, I guess."

"That's bad, Ma. I'll have to look into that."

"What's bad about it? It's always been all right for *you* to have girls, and Lord knows you've had more than your share of 'em!"

Cordell smiled. "I wouldn't say that, Ma. But Clem's different—you know, innocent-like. What about Sue Ellen? Anybody comin' courtin' these days?"

"What do you expect? She's a mighty pretty girl, son. You can't keep her caged up all her life, Ash!"

"Who is it, Ma?" Cordell's tanned face was solemn and stern.

Ma Muller turned to Tannehill. "Listen to him! Askin' questions after he's been gallivantin' from here to breakfast all over creation. I'm the one should be askin' questions, not him!" She placed her hand on Cordell's shoulder. "They've got lives of their own to lead, Ash. You always lived yours the way you wanted to. Why don't you leave them alone?"

"They'll get hurt," Cordell said. "I don't get hurt, Ma, but they will."

"Everybody gets hurt," said Ma Muller. "Drink up now, boys, and get this food into you. Make you feel better, Ash."

"I'm all right, Ma." He smiled warmly up at her, but she knew he wasn't all right. His mother had told Ash to take care of them, and he meant to do so, insofar as he could, as long as he lived. Ma wondered if he'd heard rumors about his sister and Gene Garriott. Undoubtedly he had, the way gossip got around, as if the winds carried it to every corner of the vast Carikaree Basin.

It was always good to get back here and see Ma Muller, but the homecoming wasn't what it should have been for Ash Cordell. Unreasonably, he felt that Sue Ellen and Clem should have been there to greet him, even though they were unaware of his coming. He knew now that Bob Woodlee had been telling the truth. At this moment, his sister was somewhere with Gene Garriott and Clem was probably with some dance hall girl. It made Ash ill, and spoiled the taste of the fine steak and hashed brown potatoes.

Ma and Tan tried to jolly him out of it, and Ash made a pretense of gaiety, but nobody was fooled by it. Afterward, Ma Muller brought them a handful of long thin cigars from the lobby case, and Cordell and Tannehill did up the dishes for her. Then they carried hot water up to the room that Ma always reserved for them. After bathing, shaving, and changing into clean clothes, they felt and looked a great deal better.

"A handsome pair of hellions," Ma Muller remarked, when they reappeared downstairs in the lobby. "If I was younger, and twins, I'd put an end to your footloose ways. Don't go down there and shoot up the town now, boys."

Leaving the front porch, they descended the grade to the level of Western Avenue, which paralleled the hotel gallery, and crossed into the lighted length of Front Street, stretching straight ahead of them between homes and business buildings. This end of the street was quiet, the night life area restricted mainly to the eastern side of town. Tramping the boardwalk, they passed under the wooden awnings of familiar darkened stores and came to the adobe-block bank. Court Street branched to the right with its big courthouse and trim white church. Across on the left loomed Murphy's Market, dwarfing the other shops.

They went on past other false-fronted stores, raucous saloons, and Pruett's saddle and harness shop. Here the street was gaudy with lights and dinning noisily, the hitch-racks lined with horses and wagons, the usual loafers loitering in the shadows. The Longhorn Saloon was before them. Over on the left were the Golden Wheel gambling emporium and the Rio Belle dance hall.

They pushed the swing doors into the Longhorn, spoke to acquaintances here and there, and scanned the smoky interior for hostile riders from Hatchet. Not seeing any, they drifted into the long bar and settled comfortably against it, their eyes watching the back-bar mirror. Bartender Koney hailed them with casual good cheer and set up a bottle and two small glasses.

"Any Hatchet in town tonight?" asked Cordell.

"Kyler was in earlier with Laidlaw and Hamrick. Ain't seen anybody else."

"Clem been around, Koney?"

The little bartender looked slightly uncomfortable. "Not in here, Ash. Might be over to the Rio. You boys are lookin' fit and sharp."

"Hard steady work," drawled Tannehill. "That's the secret."

"Ha, ha," Koney said, expressionless, his narrow balding head moistly aglitter. "You got any more funny stories?" He leaned across toward them. "Heard the huntin' was pretty good out Trelhaven way."

"Not bad, Koney," said Cordell.

"They're a little thicker around these parts. A man could almost close his eyes and hit one of 'em any time. I guess you boys know where I stand on the matter."

"Sure, Koney, and we're glad to know it."

Koney pushed their money back across the

wood, poured them another round, and moved away down the bar. They saluted him in the mirror, tossed off the drinks, and went outside. After surveying the street with slow care, they crossed diagonally toward the Rio Belle, glancing at the horses racked there. Three of them bore the Hatchet brand, and a sudden fear chilled Ash Cordell. They might figure on taking his brother Clement, to even up for Thorner and Skowron. That would be like Kyler Garriott. Then he recalled that Clem didn't pack a gun, unless he'd started to recently. Even Kyler would hesitate about throwing down on an unarmed man.

The music hit them in the face with its brassy blare, and they saw that the floor was crowded with gaily twirling couples, the bright dresses of the girls in contrast to the somber garb of the men. Standing at the rail, Cordell and Tannehill looked the place over, not seeing Clem at first. Two house girls came over with false smiles of welcome, and Tannehill grinned at them, but Cordell waved them away without a glance. Then he spotted Kyler Garriott at the bar, Hamrick and Laidlaw on either side of him.

Kyler was backed against the wood with a drink in his hand, a towering lanky figure with wide spare shoulders. He was dressed in black, except for a white hat and neckpiece, the two bone-handled guns and silver-ornamented boots. His head was rather small, sleek and black under the pushed-back hat, with an odd reptilian thrust to it. Kyler Garriott was watching a corner of the dance floor, his thin ferret-face drawn sharper than ever, his black eyes narrowed and shining with an oily luster. He looked deadly, and he was. Kyler was rated superior to any of the professional gunmen his father hired, except possibly the mysterious, seldom seen Hodkey.

The two men with him were just about as expert with their guns. Laidlaw looked like anything but a killer. He was slim and blond, a smiling boy with a smooth clear face that was almost girlish, almost beautiful. They called him Pretty Boy, and there was no disparagement in the term. His innocent delicate appearance had led many hard-case strangers into insulting him, calling him, reaching—and thereby committing suicide.

Hamrick was quite the opposite, broad, massive and burly, a bull of a man with a fighting bull's ferocity, courage and driving power. For variety, it was said, Hamrick sometimes killed opponents with his bare hands. He had shaggy auburn hair and a broad flat face, broken-nosed, seamed with scars, brutal-jawed. Red Hamrick was in no way pretty but, like Laidlaw, he ranked with the top gun-sharps of Hatchet.

Cordell followed Kyler Garriott's concentrated gaze and located the couple he was staring at, just as Tannehill clutched Cord's arm, swearing and pointing to the same corner. The man was Clem, and the girl was Nita Dell, perky and flirty, vivid and voluptuous. Ash Cordell cursed viciously, his biceps swelling taut under Tan's fingers.

"That poor kid," murmured Ash. "With a woman like that, a real little beast. What chance would Clem have?"

"She's sure givin' him the treatment," Tannehill drawled. "I wonder how many men she's got killed in her time?"

"It's a good thing we rode this way, Tan," said Ash Cordell. "I'm goin' over there. Cover my back, Tanny."

"Sure, Cord. I got those three at the bar tagged."

Ash slipped easily through the whirling couples, weaving his way toward that far corner. The music ceased before he got there, but Nita Dell remained close to Clem, smiling up at him with pouted crimson lips, her dark eyes filled with a swooning look, her full body swaying seductively. Clem acted stunned, bedazzled and wholly entranced. The sight of him that way with a woman like Nita set off a blazing bursting rage in Ash Cordell.

Clement, surprised and a bit guilty, looked up at his big brother's approach. He was a stocky-built young man with a clean, frank, boyish face, wavy brown hair, darker than Ash's, and large brown eyes of velvet softness. His features were straight and regular, and there was a look of shining cleanness about him.

"Why, Ash," he said, embarrassed but glad as he

reached out a hand. "It's good to see you back, Ash. Here, I want you to meet—"

"We've met, Clem," said Ash, shaking his hand and staring steadily at the girl, her musky perfume reminding him of two men lying in a dim powder-reeking hotel corridor. "Can I have the next dance?"

"Sure, Ash." Clem looked from one to the other. "Go right ahead."

"Have you got a ticket, Cord?" asked Nita tauntingly.

"I'll use one of Clem's."

"In Trelhaven you wouldn't dance at all."

"I dance better here maybe."

Nita Dell smiled sweetly at him. "I didn't expect to see you again so soon, Cord."

"Or maybe never," Ash Cordell said.

The music was starting up when Kyler Garriott arrived, ignoring the brothers at first, eyeing the girl with dark menace. "This is my dance, Nita."

"You're a little late, Kyler." She was already in Ash's formal embrace, and they were circling slowly out of the corner, to the tune of *Gathering the Myrtle with Mary*. Kyler watched them a moment, and then turned on Clem, his weasel-face thrusting sharply down at the smaller man.

"I told you to keep away from her, Clem."

Clem smiled with sober good nature. "I'm not takin' orders from you, Kyler. I'll stay away when Nita tells me to herself."

Kyler stood with habitual Garriott arrogance, hands on hips and elbows spread wide, taller than Ash or anybody else on the floor, an insolent smile on his narrow bony face. He and Clem were of an age, as was the case with Gene Garriott and Ash, but Kyler seemed much older, a hard-bitten ïman of the world towering over a simple naïve boy.

"It's too bad you never grew up enough to carry a gun, Clem," said Kyler.

"I've got one," Clem said quietly. "If I have to, I can use it."

"You're liable to have to, boy. I'm gettin' sick of havin' you Cordells cuttin' in on my women. Ash moved in on Laura Delsing, and now you're hornin' in on Nita. I ought to beat your curly head off, boy."

"You should've tried it before Ash got back."

Kyler laughed contemptuously. "You goin' to spend all your life hidin' behind your big brother's back? He sure must get tired of nurse-maidin' a pup like you!"

Clem's cheeks colored hotly. "I'll wear that gun for you hereafter, Kyler. I don't take that kind of talk from anybody."

"That's good," Kyler Garriott said. "When I see you with a gun on, Clem, you're dead."

Kyler laughed again and strode away, elbowing and shouldering people aside as he swaggered back toward the bar, where Hamrick and Laidlaw had been observing the scene while Tannehill kept an eye on them. Watching Kyler's lanky high-shouldered back, Clement Cordell felt cold and shaken, his legs trembling so that he was thankful to find an empty chair at a nearby table. He had been practicing with a six-gun, but he'd never fired at any living thing. He didn't even like to think about it. On the other hand, Clem couldn't much longer endure being despised as a weakling and coward, snickered at as Ash Cordell's craven little brother. Better to die than go on being an object of ridicule and scorn, a complete nonentity.

Only Nita Dell believed in him, and made Clem feel like a man of stature and significance, full-grown and brave and able to stand up among other men. Nita had a worshipful way of looking up at him that filled Clem with confidence and self-esteem. When she looked at him that way, Clem felt capable of facing anybody and doing anything.

On the dance floor, Nita Dell was gazing up at his brother now with an archly challenging expression. "Did you see Bob Woodlee before you left Trelhaven?" she asked guilelessly.

"Yes, but I didn't kill him or let him kill me. Sorry to disappoint you."

She was properly indignant. "What in the world are you talking about?"

"You drove Woodlee crazy," Ash Cordell said coldly. "Now you're workin' on my brother. But

79

you're all done there, Nita. You aren't goin' to see any more of Clem."

"Is that so?" Nita Dell demanded with brazen defiance. "Who are you to order me around? Clem's of age and I happen to like him. He's a lot better-looking than you are, big brother. Maybe that's why you always tromped him down, treated him like a baby."

"I'm not very pretty," smiled Ash. "Neither is Kyler Garriott."

Nita laughed. "But Kyler's rich. Kyler's got all kinds of money!"

Ash Cordell looked down at her sensual face. "There ought to be a law against women like you." In time to the jangling music, he was swinging her gradually nearer the bar.

"I'm a naughty girl," she giggled, "but I can be awful nice, Cord. I know how to make a man mighty happy!"

"And mighty dead," Ash Cordell said grimly, spinning her ever closer to the opening in the rail before the bar. The Hatchet trio watched them across the railing, while Tannehill and Clem drifted in that direction.

"What a thing to say!" exclaimed the girl. "I can be real sweet to a man, Cord, all sugar and spice."

"Be sweet to Kyler then!" Ash said, turning her loose and swinging her around by the wrist, flinging her on toward the three Garriott men at the bar.

Kyler caught her, his drink splashing over both of them. Letting go of Nita then, Kyler smashed his glass on the floor and strode straight at Cordell, halting in a tall stark stance ten feet in front of Ash, who said mildly:

"There she is, Kyler. Ride closer herd on her, if you want to hold onto her. And keep her off my brother's neck."

"You're askin' for it, Cord," said Kyler Garriott. "You been askin' for it a long time now." The two Hatchet men stepped up on either side of him, Laidlaw slender and smiling sunnily, Hamrick bulky and glowering.

"Let's have it then," Ash Cordell said. "You've got your usual odds, Kyler."

Tannehill sauntered alongside of Ash, long and loose-limbed with an amber glint in his eyes, a reckless grin curving his lips. "Evens them up some, Cord," he drawled. "Makes 'em too even for Hatchet." And Clem moved in at Tannehill's shoulder, weaponless but determined to stand by them.

Couples stopped dancing to stare at this tense tableau, the music broke off discordantly, and people scrambled out of the line of fire. Three against three they faced one another in the smoke-layered lamplight, but there were six guns on the Hatchet side and only two showing for the Cordells. Silent and motionless they stood there, hatred a tangible evil thing between the two lines, until the strain became unbearable. Then a genial slurring voice broke it.

"What's all the fuss here? This ain't no way to enjoy a dance, boys." Sheriff Rubeling shook his head sorrowfully. "Ash, I didn't know you was back home. You and trouble are still ridin' together, I see."

"The name's Tannehill, Rube," grinned Tan in wry protest.

"Didn't mean you exactly, Tan. Trouble in general just naturally seems to trail Ash around. Now you Hatchet boys stand back to the bar, and I'll take a walk in the air with these three boys." He signaled the orchestra to strike up the music, and motioned the dancers back into action. Sheriff Rubeling was a commanding figure, a huge rawboned man even taller than Kyler, with the battle-scarred face of a hawk, the piercing eyes of an eagle. His mouth was like a steel trap, and a large chew of tobacco bulged one seamed leathery cheek.

Clem stood rooted gazing at Nita Dell, but her luminous dark eyes were fixed on Kyler Garriott, blind to everything else. Ash struck him sharply on the shoulder, and Clem turned numbly away after the high form of the sheriff. Kyler and his two gunmen watched them venomously all the way out.

Rubeling paused thoughtfully on the slat walk outside. "I'll buy you boys a drink in the

Longhorn. Ash, what is this feelin' you've got against the Garriotts? It's goin' to bring on killin' in time, Ash, and it don't seem right, after old Gurney took you folks in and raised you like his own kids on Hatchet. It worries me considerable, Ash, and it has for a long time. You ought to be friendly, or at least sociable with the Garriotts, seein' as how Sue Ellen and Gene are goin' steady together."

"Never, Rube," said Ash Cordell, his low voice charged with emotion. "I'm goin' to bust that up. I won't have my sister marry a Garriott."

"Listen, Ash, I'm not makin' any brief for Gurney and Kyler, but Gene's a whole lot different. So far as I know Gene never warred on the nesters, or ran with the gun-pack at all. I don't see where a girl hereabouts could do much better than Gene, honest I don't!"

"He's a Garriott, and that's enough. He's not for Sue Ellen."

"Curses and damnation, man!" growled Sheriff Rubeling. "If the girl loves Gene, you can't change it or stop it."

"Yes, I can, Rube," said Ash gently. "And I sure as the devil will."

"What's wrong with Gene Garriott, outside of your not likin' him?"

"He's no good. None of the Garriotts are any good. Rich and big and powerful, yes, but rotten inside, rotten way through. You know what

83

they've done, Rube, as well as I do. The home-steaders they've driven off and burned out and killed. The herds they've stolen, the land they've grabbed, the small ranches they've swallowed up. The families they've split and broken and ruined."

"You got proof of all that, Ash?" inquired Rubeling dryly.

"I've seen some things and heard a lot of others. I saw what they did to the Woodlees up on the Bittersweet. Shot down the father and mother, burned the house with them in it, wounded and screamin'. Flogged young Woody half to death."

Rubeling spat and swallowed. "That was a bad one, I know, but we had no proof who did it. There's always talk against people like the Garriotts. The law can't go on guesswork or hearsay, Ash."

"I'm not blamin' you or your office, Rube. I know how things are."

"Accordin' to what you say, boy, I ain't doin' my duty here."

"I'm not sayin' that, Rube," protested Ash Cordell. "I do say the Garriotts get away with a lot that other folks couldn't. Because they own the whole east end of the valley, because they're so big and wealthy and strong. It's like they're beyond the law."

There was restrained anger in the sheriff's reply:

"Nobody's beyond the law! Seems to me you and Tan got off pretty easy over in Trelhaven, when it comes to that."

"It was self-defense, Rube. They climbed us and we had to shoot or die. But if it happened here, we'd have been tried for murder, I reckon, if we weren't hung before the trial."

"You mean this is a Garriott town, and I'm a Garriott man?"

Ash Cordell shook his head. "I don't think you're a Garriott man at heart, Rube. But your hands are pretty well tied, aren't they?"

"In public office, any man's hands are tied to some extent, I suppose," Rubeling said wearily, glumly. "I can't stop all the feudin' and fightin' in the Carikaree. What do you want me to do, Ash?" He seemed abruptly old and tired, his great height diminished, the hawklike face sunken with sadness.

Ash smiled gravely. "Well, you *could* deputize Tan and me."

Rubeling spat a stream of tobacco juice. "I got all the deputies I can carry, and you know it, Ash. Besides, you two boys got a reputation for trouble-makin' that don't exactly fit behind a badge."

"And Hatchet wouldn't stand for it either, Rube," needled Ash.

"Hot blazes and corruption!" the sheriff said. "I've got a full crew of deputies, and that's all there is to it."

"Sure, and not a one of 'em would lift a gun against the Garriotts! Not even if they caught 'em changin' a brand, holdin' up a stage, or robbin' the bank." Ash was supremely scornful.

"Now I got a couple or three pretty good boys, Ash. You take Paynter and Maddern and Shokes. They wouldn't care much for that kind of talk, even from you, Ash."

Ash Cordell laughed. "You can tell 'em I said it, Rube. They know where I live."

"You're too tough for your own good, son," grumbled Rubeling, and sighed deeply. "Let's get to that drink in the Longhorn. All this gabbin' grows a thirst."

"One thing I wish you'd bear in mind, Rube," said Ash. "Hatchet's been threatenin' Dan Delsing on Wagon Mound."

Rubeling spat viciously. "Anybody that harms the Delsings is in trouble with me, Ash, Garriotts or whatever they are!"

Chapter VI

Cadmus Flats slumbered under the moon. The Hillhouse Hotel was also asleep on its westerly bench, except for Ash Cordell, who sat alone in the darkened lobby. Ma Muller and her employees and patrons had long since retired. Clem and Tannehill had finally gone up to bed, at Ash's insistence. Lounging in a deep leather chair before the large plate glass window, Ash Cordell smoked a cigar and watched the moonlight gild the roof-tops of the town with silver. He was waiting for his sister Sue Ellen and Gene Garriott. His lazy slouching attitude belied the emotions that were seething within him.

He could see straight down the empty moonlit expanse of Front Street, almost to the East Bridge over the Carikaree River, and the road that led eastward past Blue Butte to Hatchet. To the left, North Bridge was visible, and beyond it the trail running northeast to Chimney Rocks and Wagon Mound. To the right, he saw the landmarks of Court Street, the bulk of the courthouse, the square belfry and tapering spire of the church, that had been designed after the white churches of New England and looked a bit out of place in this Western community.

Ash Cordell perceived these things only abstractedly, for his mind had gone back to the youthful days on Hatchet. Even seventeen years ago the ranch had been enormous, a veritable town in itself, centered about the Big House, a great limestone structure. There were immense frame barns and stables, long bunkhouses of adobe and wood, rows of cabins for privileged employees with families, a large cookshack and dining hall, and an extensive array of corrals, sheds and outbuildings. Hatchet had its own general store, saloon, blacksmith shop, and even a schoolhouse that also served as a church. To children reared in a mountain wilderness, it seemed at first like a crowded, noisy, swarming city, overwhelming and bewildering them.

Old Gurney Garriott gave them rooms in the Big House, and they took their meals with the family. Gurney and his tall, cold, patrician wife obviously meant to raise them impartially with their own sons, but it never quite came off that way. They went to school and played with the Garriott boys and other Hatchet children, and apparently received the same consideration and treatment, privileges and discipline that Gene and Kyler did. But there was natural and inevitable differentiation, and Ash never liked it or felt at home there. The younger Cordells, remembering little of their previous years, accepted this new order of things much easier and better than Ash was able to.

Ash knew that they didn't really fit or belong there; they were more or less intruders, like poor relations taken into a wealthy household. In the Big House, they were never truly welcomed by either the family or the servants, nor did they belong to the bunkhouses and outer menage. They were in the middle, unwanted, no place for them on any side. Gurney, ruthless and domineering, was too busy building his empire to spare any time for youngsters, even his own. Mrs. Garriott, a bloodless stylized aristocrat from the East, had no warmth or affection for the orphans, no feeling at all other than a vague distaste.

Gene and Kyler were forever taunting them: "You ain't Garriotts! You ain't nobody! You're just found kids!" And Ash was always fighting them, one at a time or both together, taking his lickings and going back for more. Occasionally Clem pitched in, but he wasn't much help, and Ash was seldom without blackened eyes, cut lips, swollen nose, facial abrasions and cranial lumps. Ash never cried or complained, and even when questioned by Gurney and his wife he remained stubbornly silent, refusing to blame the Garriott brothers. Ash was getting tougher and stronger all the while. At fifteen or sixteen, Gene had trouble whipping him alone, despite Gene's advantage in size, and generally Kyler joined in to make sure that Ash got a sound drubbing.

Ash Cordell had hated the Garriott boys instinctively from the start, and this hatred increased with every thrashing he took at their hands. At seventeen, Ash was becoming very hard to handle—unruly, rebellious and wild as a mustang, at home, in school and abroad. When Gurney called him onto the carpet, Ash lashed out at him: "Who am I? Who were my folks? What happened up in the mountains? I want to know, I've got to know!" Old Gurney was surprisingly gentle and kind on that occasion, but he hadn't been able to furnish any information. He had never heard of the Cordell family; didn't even know which mountains they had come out of. Gurney tried to soothe the boy, advising him to forget all about the tragic past and concentrate on living his own life.

"You're good, Ash, and you can go a long way on Hatchet," said Gurney. "You can already ride and rope and shoot better than some of my regular hands. It seems to come natural to you, boy. You can be a tophand at twenty-one, the rate you're comin' along, and a wagon boss or better at twenty-five."

But Ash didn't care about his future prospects. He wanted to learn the story of his family and himself, establish an identity and a background, feel whole and complete and normal. The one thing he did like about Hatchet, however, was the opportunity to train and develop himself in the handling of horses and cattle, ropes and guns. At eighteen, Ash Cordell was an expert at cutting, roping and branding. He could twist broncs in the breaking corral, build a point and ride it on the trail-drives to the railhead, make river crossings with a herd. He read sign like an Indian scout on the trail, and handled guns as if he'd been born with a Colt in his clasp.

Ash was eighteen when he went back to the

schoolhouse one afternoon to get a book he had forgotten, and found Sue Ellen struggling in the arms of Gene Garriott, who was so engrossed in kissing the fourteen-year-old girl that he never heard Ash come in. Ripping them apart, Ash spun Gene around, smashed him in the face, and went after the bigger boy with wildcat fury. That was the first time Ash ever beat Gene, and he did a beautiful job of it, belting him all over the room, bouncing him off the walls, knocking him down, never stopping until Gene was unconscious on the floor, a battered bleeding hulk.

That evening old Gurney called Ash into his office, with the intention of taking a quirt to him, but when Ash saw him pick up the whip he pulled a gun out of his waistband. Gurney, realizing that the boy would use the gun if he had to, flung the quirt down and ordered Ash off the premises, once and for all.

"Why, sure," Ash said, smiling thinly. "Nothin' I'd like better than to get the stink of Hatchet out of my head. I'll be back for my brother and sister before long, and if Gene has laid so much as a finger on Sue Ellen, I'll kill him! And I'll kill you or anybody else that tries to stop me!"

"You're goin' to end up with a rope around your neck, boy," Gurney told him.

"Maybe so. But there won't be any Garriotts left around to see it."

"How can you feel that way toward us, boy?

After all we've done for you and your brother and sister."

"I don't rightly know," Ash Cordell said gravely. "But I got a feelin' you've done us more harm than you can ever make up for."

"What do you mean, you young idiot?"

"You know what happened to our folks, and you know who did it."

Old Gurney had raged and cursed at this. "How would I know, you mad ungrateful dog? I never set eyes on your folks. I don't know anybody that ever did. For all I know, and from the way you act, you might've been spawned of a mountain lion. Get out now and stay out of my sight, before I have you shot like the back-bitin' coyote you are!"

"Gladly," said Ash. "But see that my sister and brother are treated right, mister!"

Ash had said his good-byes, gathered his gear, and gone to the stable for the horse Gurney had given him, when the old monarch changed his mind and decided to have the boy held. Two gunhands went out to stop young Cordell, but Ash had got the drop on them, took their gun-belts, and went out of Hatchet at a wild gallop. Gurney ordered a pursuit, and then canceled it before the men could saddle up. There'd be plenty of time to take that crazy kid, if he had to be taken. And Gurney knew it would come to that eventually.
So Ash Cordell had broken loose on his own at eighteen, and not long after that Ma Muller had

legally adopted the three Cordells, a move that Gurney never made. And Sheriff Rubeling had transferred Sue Ellen and Clement from Hatchet to the Hillhouse in Cadmus Flats.

At times Ash thought he should have been somewhat grateful to the Garriotts, after all, for with all its drawbacks Hatchet had done a lot for the Cordell children. They had been educated there, better than most in this frontier land. They had been well fed and well clothed, taught polite company manners, how to talk and act and dress. They had grown up strong and straight and healthy, and Ash, at least, had acquired a trade there that fitted him for life in the West.

But always inside him was that instinctive hatred and distrust of the Garriotts, and the firm belief that there was some ulterior and evil motive behind Gurney's philanthropy. . . .

Now shadows fell across the broad porch steps, and Ash Cordell straightened in his chair. Sue Ellen and Gene Garriott came into view, the girl looking small and dainty beside the hulking frame of the man. Ash could see them clearly in the moonlight, their arms linked, their faces turned raptly to one another, smiling, happy and intimate. Ash's fists knotted until his arms ached numbly to the elbow, and his teeth bit way through the cigar.

Gene had grown big and broad and powerful, like old Gurney, and he looked handsome, with black curls tousled on his forehead, his features straight, strong and regular, his smile laden with the Garriott charm that Kyler had missed out on entirely. They kissed and turned to look at the moonlit town, their arms around each other, and Ash Cordell winced as if he had been struck across the face.

Slowly, reluctant to part, they entered the dark lobby and paused for a farewell embrace. Ash came to his feet and dropped the mangled cigar butt, feeling strangely naked without the gun-belt dragging on his hips. He had hung up the gun because he didn't want to kill Gene Garriott— yet. In deference to his sister, Ash meant to give Gene a chance. Startled, the couple separated and whirled staring, as he strode toward them in the faint light.

"Ash!" cried Sue Ellen, running to him and throwing her arms about his neck, raising her face to him.

But her brother turned his head before her lips reached his mouth. "Not after him, Sue."

"Oh, Ash!" she sighed, desperate and forlorn. "Please, Ash, don't—"

But Ash Cordell had set her aside and was moving on toward Gene Garriott, who stood waiting and watchful, his boots apart and his hands half lifted, ready for anything. Gene's smile was gone, and muscles bunched along his heavy jawbones; his eyes were darkly intense. He wore a beautifully tailored suit of rich gray broadcloth. There was no gun in sight, but he probably had one in a shoulder holster.

"You know what happened the last few times I found you two together," Ash said. "It won't happen tonight—if you get out, Gene, and never come back."

"It's no use, Ash." Gene shook his curly head. "You aren't running our lives any more. This is our affair, Sue's and mine. You've got nothing to say about it. We're going to get married soon."

"You'll never live that long," Ash Cordell told him. "You'd better forget all about it, Gene. Stick to those half-breed girls you and Kyler have out Blue Butte way."

Gene Garriott's right hand thrust toward his left armpit.

"I haven't got a gun on," Ash said calmly. "I was afraid I'd kill you, Gene, if I wore a gun."

"Well, I couldn't shoot you in front of your sister anyway. I imagine you figured on that too, Ash." He took off the gray coat, unhooked the shoulder holster, and tossed them into the nearest chair. "I don't need a gun either. You'll never whip me again, Ash. But I suppose you'll insist on trying."

Sue Ellen ran and clung to Gene Garriott. "No, no, no!" she implored. "Please go, Gene, and let me talk to Ash. Don't fight here, Gene, please don't!"

"Might as well be here and now," Gene said grimly, forcing her gently aside. "There are more

95

sensible civilized ways, but none that Ash under-stands."

Ash Cordell laughed mockingly. "Sensible and civilized, the way you Garriotts deal with little homesteaders and small ranchers? Come on, you hypocrite; put up your hands!"

"I never held with a lot of things Hatchet does. I never took part in any of those range wars, Ash. But I'm ready to fight you, if you're bound to have it."

"You're noble, Gene," said Ash Cordell, reaching out with casual contempt and slapping that high handsome face.

It was a mistake, for Gene Garriott struck with sudden speed as Ash slapped him, landing heavily on the jaw, rocking Ash's head back, stunning and staggering him. Before Cordell could recover, Gene was on top of him, slugging hard, driving him back with unleashed fury. Garriott was three inches taller and thirty pounds heavier, fast for a man of his size, and Ash couldn't hold him off long enough to regain his equilibrium.

Something caught the back of Cordell's legs and he went over backward, the floor smashing his shoulders and beating the breath from his lungs. Gene was hurtling down on top of him, but Ash got his legs up in time to catch that ponderous weight on his boots and kick Gene on overhead to fall with a jarring crash that shook the entire building. Rolling and springing catlike to his feet,

Cordell was up first and waiting in a balanced crouch, waiting until Garriott came up, then driving in and hitting him, left and right to the face, lifting Gene back against the lobby counter, dropping him heavily at the foot of it.

Garriott floundered there, shaken and hurt as Ash had been, but thrashing out with his booted legs as Cordell closed in. Ash took one bootheel on the kneecap, the other in the groin, and stumbled off in crippled agony. Gene swung onto his hands and knees, and came in a low sweeping rush along the floor. Still bent with cramping pain, Cordell lifted his knee wickedly into that oncoming face and clubbed both fists to the sides of the head. Garriott stopped short and crumpled back, gasping and groaning, but Ash was too racked with the anguish in his groin to follow up the advantage.

Scrabbling frantically on the hardwood boards, Gene Garriott reared up and rushed forward, mighty arms flailing. Ducking in under, Ash Cordell ripped both hands into the waistline, sinking them deep, and Gene's breath sobbed raggedly out as he doubled with the jolting impacts.

Straightening up and standing off, Cordell measured his enemy with cold precision, stabbing him upright with a left, pouring all his coordinated power into a whipping overhand right. It landed with a brutal smash, and Ash felt the shock way to his shoulder. Garriott's curly head jerked far back and his body followed it down, bouncing on the floor, skidding on his shoulders until his skull thumped the baseboard of the office desk.

"That's enough, Ash!" cried Sue Ellen, huddled on the wall.

"Maybe," panted Cordell. "Maybe not." He was swaying slightly himself, his lungs pumping and his heart hammering, the pain still knifing through his groin and kneecap. He tasted blood in his mouth, and his face felt numbed and enormously swollen. His left eye was bruised and closing, and his hands ached as if the knuckle-bones were splintered.

It would have been enough for most men, but Gene Garriott was getting up, slowly and uncertainly, supporting himself on the counter, his battered face glistening darkly with blood. Ash Cordell waited, needing the rest and giving a game opponent a chance to recover. Garriott hurled himself forward all at once, and Ash met him squarely, slamming away until their weary arms interlocked. Clinching and grappling, they wrestled back and forth, upsetting chairs and tables. Garriott brought a knee up into Cordell's aching abdomen, and Ash butted his head viciously into Gene's chin.

They broke and circled groggily. Garriott swung round-armed, but Cordell was sliding inside and slashing straight away, beating the

98

giant back. A left lashed Gene against the wall; his hands dropped as he bounced forward again. Ash hooked him left and right, and the big man tottered on jacking knees. Ash Cordell threw everything into a shattering right. Gene Garriott stiffened up high, pawing the air blindly, and toppled forward with the slow majestic finality of a great tree chopped down, landing on his bloody face and shuddering into stillness.

"No more, Ash, no more!" pleaded Sue Ellen, flinging herself frantically on her brother. "Don't touch him again, Ash. I'll—I'll hate you, if you do!"

Ash looked at her in dull surprise. "Reckon—that's—enough," he gasped painfully, shaking his sweaty head and massaging his raw puffed knuckles, feeling weak and sick now that it was over. Sue Ellen ran and knelt beside Gene, then hurried to the kitchen and came back with a basin of water and a towel. Ash walked around in slow uneven circles while she bathed Garriott's face and head, thinking bitterly: She went right to him. She doesn't care if I'm hurt or not. She's in love with that Garriott. Why do things have to happen like that? All the men in the world, and she has to pick him.

Gene was soon on his feet and mumbling through mashed, lacerated lips: "All right, Ash, you won. But it won't do you any good. You can't keep me away from Sue."

"I'll kill you then," Ash Cordell said, quiet and deadly.

"You think you're bullet-proof?" Gene asked through the blood-soaked towel.

"Enough to stand up against any Garriott."

"You can't break this up, Ash. Nothing can—ever."

"The next time it'll be with guns," Ash told him. "The next time I see you, start reachin'."

Sue Ellen spoke, quite evenly in spite of her weeping: "Ash, will you please leave us alone now? You whipped him. You've done enough. You should be satisfied, Ash."

"All right, Sue," he said flatly. "But tell him not to come back—while I'm here. I've threatened before. Next time I'll shoot him." Ash Cordell crossed to the stairway and started climbing, holding onto the banister and lifting one foot after the other, feeling utterly spent and exhausted, torn and twisted and unhappy inside. There had been no satisfaction in beating Gene this time, not with Sue Ellen loving him, standing with him against her brother.

Ma Muller was waiting in the upstairs corridor with a lamp in her hand, an expression of suffering on her face. She had been making the rounds, calming and reassuring the disturbed guests, urging them to return to bed and pay no attention to the boys rough-housing around downstairs.

"So you had to go and do it?" she murmured reproachfully. "Look at your face and hands. You're a mess! Oh, Ash, why don't you let them alone?"

"No Garriott's goin' to have my sister."

"You can't run everythin', Ash boy. You can't control people's lives and loves to suit yourself. You aren't God!"

"No, Ma," said Ash Cordell, smiling a bleak distorted smile through the blood and sweat. "Not even close, Ma. But I got somethin' to say about my own sister."

"Yes, but not that much."

He bent and brushed his sore mouth across her gray hair. "Go to bed now, Ma, and stop frettin'. Nobody's hurt—much. No real damage done."

But there will be if you keep on, Ash boy, she thought miserably, watching his rangy, broad-shouldered figure move limping down the hall-way, love and pain and fear in her tired blue eyes. There'll be death and destruction all through the Carikaree.

Chapter VII

Things were a bit strained, awkward and unpleasant in the Hillhouse Hotel. There had been a drastic change during Ash's latest absence. Sue Ellen and Clement had grown up and away from him. The brawl with Gene Garriott had left a wide and serious breach between Sue and Ash, while Clem was withdrawn, preoccupied and resentful over the Nita Dell matter. Hillhouse wasn't the same homelike place at all, with constant worry etching Ma Muller's face, and Ash Cordell was saddened and lonely, missing Laura Delsing more than ever. He supposed it was inevitable for brothers and sisters to drift apart as the years passed, but that didn't lesson the hurt it brought to Ash.

On this morning, Ash Cordell was wandering in moody disconsolateness about the hotel and the grounds of the small plateau. Tannehill, oppressed by the strained relations at the hotel, had wandered downtown, maybe to try his luck with a few turns at the Golden Wheel. Ma Muller and Sue Ellen were busy with their duties within the establishment, and Clem had disappeared. Ash paced outside through sunlight and shadow, a tall, somber, brooding figure.

Restless and irritable, Ash wished he and Tan had gone ahead into the Madrelinos to search for Cathedral Valley. Coming back to Cadmus had served no purpose, other than to estrange himself from his sister and brother. Sue Ellen had no intention of giving up Gene Garriott, and Clem would probably slip back to the Rio Belle after Nita Dell at the first opportunity. Ash Cordell's whole existence suddenly seemed empty and pointless, without meaning or purpose. He might as well leave Sue and Clem to their fates, as they wanted it, and continue his quest for that lost upland valley. At least when he was hunting for that his life had some direction and objective.

"What you need is a job, Ash boy," Ma Muller had told him.

Ash had shaken his bronze-colored head. "I wasn't cut out to work for other men and take orders all my life, Ma. I wouldn't mind workin' for myself now."

"You're proud as Lucifer and twice as independent!" Ma had said. "You've got to have a stake, Ash, in order to work for yourself."

"That's what's the matter, Ma," grinned Ash wryly.

Ash sauntered back into the dusty dimness of the stable, with its smell of hay and horses and leather. Catching a flicker of motion in the rear, he drifted that way and came upon Clement, a gun-belt strapped on, practicing his draw. Clem turned, startled and angered, coloring and smiling sheepishly when he saw his big brother there watching him.

"It's better if you do some shootin' at the end of your draw, Clem," said Ash kindly. "More practical that way."

"Can't afford to waste shells," Clem protested, painfully embarrassed. "Just limberin' up anyway, Ash."

"That isn't for you, Clem. That's my line, kid, and about all I'm good for. You aren't plannin' to pack a gun around, are you?"

"Looks like I'll have to, Ash. Unless I want Kyler Garriott runnin' me right out of town."

"Listen, Clem, and don't get mad," Ash said patiently. "That Nita Dell is no darn good, and I know it for a fact. You heard about the shootin' in Trelhaven? She started that deliberate, settin' Tan and me up for the Hatchet gunmen to burn down, but luck was with us. You remember Bob Woodlee? Well, she had Woody roped for fair, and he was even figurin' on marryin' her. She tried to set Woody gunnin' for me, and it almost worked out, Woody was that far gone on her. . . . Now she's leadin' you on, playin' you off against Kyler, fixin' you up to get shot, Clem. It's nothin' but a game to her, a game she's playin' for Hatchet."

"Maybe, Ash, I don't know about that. Just the same I can't let Kyler chase me out of Cadmus."

"Let me take care of the Garriotts, kid," Ash said. "Guns are my business. That Kyler's supposed to be pretty hot with a six. You can't pick up in a few weeks what a man has got in a lifetime, Clem. Look here, kid." Ash's right hand flicked and the long-barreled Colt flashed up in it, as if by magic. "You couldn't match that, Clem. But Kyler Garriott could, or come close to it."

Clem was silent, sullen, staring at the straw-littered floor.

"I don't want you wearin' a gun," Ash Cordell went on firmly. "If you put on a gun, it's suicide, Clem. Kyler won't kill you unless you're carryin' a gun."

"He'll shame me to death, though," muttered Clem, in abject misery.

"I'll tend to Kyler."

"But you won't always be here, Ash."

"I'll be here enough to handle the Garriotts."

Clement's brown eyes darkened and his fine head lifted. "A man has to stand up for himself sometime!"

"Sure, Clem," smiled Ash. "But you don't have to take a gun against a trained gun-fighter to prove yourself. Leave that for me, Clem." He slapped the boy's stalwart shoulder. "I don't want my favorite brother gettin' hurt."

Ash left the barn, and Clem went back to practicing his draw harder than ever. The smooth flawless speed of Ash's motion had discouraged him, but Clem wasn't going to back down for Kyler Garriott or anybody else. He was a good target shot, and in time he'd learn to shoot fast. Some day he'd show Ash that he was a man in his own right. His pleasant boyish face set in a grim scowl, Clem crouched and drew time and again, picturing himself wreathed in powder-smoke with Kyler Garriott, gun only halfway out, dying at his feet, and people murmuring in hoarse awed tones: "Faster'n lightning, that Clem Cordell! Faster'n his big brother Ash, even!"

In the middle of the afternoon, there was nothing to do around the hotel and Sue Ellen had signified her willingness to stay in the lobby. Clem decided to walk downtown, have a beer or two, and perhaps catch a glimpse of Nita Dell. Maybe the girl was no good, as Ash said, but she was in his blood like liquid fire, in his head like exotic perfume and pulsing music. Nothing had ever stirred and enthralled him as Nita did, made him feel so big and strong, handsome and important. She was the loveliest woman he had ever seen and he had to see her. He needed Nita Dell, and he needed the way she made him feel alive, vibrant, surging with vital power.

Ash and Tan had gone riding somewhere out in the country, and Ma Muller was taking her afternoon nap. In his room, Clem shaved and washed scrupulously, put on clean trousers, dress-up boots, and a new soft gray shirt checked with blue. He knotted a blue scarf at his throat, combed and brushed his wavy brown hair carefully, and put on his best hat. Standing in thoughtful debate, he eyed the gun-belt on its wall peg for a long irresolute space. Then, with a defiant muttered curse, he snatched down the belt and buckled it about his sturdy hips. He was too old to be treated like a kid any longer, to be ordered around by his big brother. He was twenty-five.

Sue Ellen raised her golden head from a book as Clem descended into the lobby. "My, my, you must think it's Saturday, Clement!" she chided him good-naturedly, a fond smile on her delicately chiseled face. "And what's that gun for? To impress the girls in the Rio Belle?"

"Aw, shut up, Sue," said Clem, grinning in spite of his attempt at sternness, hurrying out before she could throw any more taunts at him, eager at the sight of the sun-drenched town lying below the shelf.

Clem's brief discomfiture passed and he felt confident, almost jaunty, as he walked along Front Street, exchanging friendly cheerful greetings on the way. Clem Cordell was well liked in Cadmus, and men, women and children smiled at him and called his name as he moved in the shady arcade of wooden awnings. There were some who glanced with surprise at his holstered gun, but Clem pretended not to notice, although the heavy drag of the .44 Colt felt awkward and a trifle absurd on his right hip. It was difficult to walk naturally with that unaccustomed belt binding his hips.

Approaching the Longhorn, Clem wondered whether to drop in for a beer and a chat with Koney, or whether to cross to the dance hall and see if Nita was around. Quiet mid-afternoon was a good time to talk with her, if she wasn't still in bed or out somewhere with Kyler. He hadn't fully decided when the swing-doors of the Longhorn opened, and Laidlaw and Hamrick swaggered out and stood in front of him, blocking the plank walk and looking Clem up and down with amusement.

"He's kinda cute, Red," drawled Laidlaw, cocking his fair head and smiling his angelic smile.

"And look at that shootin' iron on him!" Hamrick laughed, tossing his auburn head on those brawny shoulders. "The kid's sure growin' up and feelin' his oats."

Clem Cordell's mouth thinned tight. "Get out of my way!"

"Just listen to that," Laidlaw said. "A real hardcase kid, if I ever saw one."

"Maybe we better move, Laid," suggested Hamrick, "before he turns that six-shooter loose on us."

"Maybe we had," agreed Laidlaw. "He's wearin'

a mean ornery look today. These young buckaroos get that way the minute they sprout a gun."

The fury was mounting red and hot in Clem Cordell, but he knew it was foolish to draw against two gun-slicks such as these two from Hatchet. He wished now he had left the gun at home. With his bare hands he could take Pretty Boy Laidlaw, he thought, although he'd have little chance against the bull-like Hamrick. He had fought with his fists on infrequent occasions, but this gun business was altogether new to him. Clem stood there in a daze, his cheeks flushed and burning, his ears rimmed with fire. He wished desperately that Ash and Tan would come along. . . . Sick and hollow inside, Clem decided that there was nothing to do but back down and walk around them into the street, much as he hated to let them force him off the sidewalk.

"He's mine, boys," rasped a voice from behind Clement, the voice of Kyler Garriott. "So you're lookin' for a fight, Clem? Well, turn around and take it, sucker!"

Clem stood frozen in his tracks, as Hamrick and Laidlaw shifted out of line. It was all prearranged, Clem realized, nerving himself to make a move. He was a dead man. An icy chill traced his spine and tightened his scalp. Teeth grating on edge, Clem Cordell wheeled to face the towering black-garbed lankiness of Kyler Garriott, his weasel-face sly, sinister and scornful.

109

"It's been a long time comin', little brother," Kyler said. "But here it is, boy. I'll give you a head start, Clem, so make your bid."

Clem Cordell made a frenzied grab for his gun, his hand stiff and jerking despite his effort to keep it smooth. Kyler's clawed left hand streaked with the speed of light, and Clem knew he was too late. Kyler was taking him left-handed, and that fleeting fact bothered Clem more than anything else. A bright roaring explosion leaped at Clem and a clublike impact smashed the middle of his body, bending and driving him back on the slats, still on his feet. Clem yanked his Colt clear of the leather but another blast caught him, rocking him backward until he brought up against an empty hitch-rack. Swaying there on the rail, Clem strained to lift his gun into line, but it was too heavy, there was no strength left in the shattered numbness of his stocky body. The gun went off, splintering the boardwalk at his feet, and Clem pitched slowly forward onto all fours, the slugs heavy and searing inside him, blood streaming and spattering on the dusty wood.

There was another blinding blaze, a thunder-clap of sound that burst the whole world open, and Clem Cordell rolled loosely onto his side, squirmed spasmodically onto his riddled belly, and lay there in a dark spreading pool, the sunshine touching his brown head with a glimmer of golden fire.

"Self-defense, boys," Kyler Garriott said to the men who had erupted from the Longhorn and other saloons and stores. "Clem reached first. He said he was comin' after me with a gun."

"A fair break, more than even," Laidlaw declared. "Kyler gave the kid a good start."

"Clem was proddin' us first," Hamrick said, "and then he went after Kyler."

"Where's Sheriff Rubeling?" asked Kyler Garriott.

"Outa town," somebody said. "And if I was you, I'd get outa town before Ash Cordell gets here!"

"Come on, boys," Kyler said, gesturing impatiently. "They know where to find us. Ash Cordell or anybody else that wants us."

Koney stood in front of his Longhorn Saloon, rubbing his bald head and watching Kyler Garriott walk away with Red Hamrick and Pretty Boy Laidlaw. He looked back to where the shocked men were shuffling about the dead body of Clem Cordell, their heads bent and their lips working dryly.

"I wouldn't want to be them," Koney said, pointing after the three Hatchet men. "Kyler Garriot's as good as dead right now, boys. As dead as young Clem here, when Ash gets word of this."

"Clem wasn't no gun-fighter," mumbled old Pruett, the saddlemaker. "Never saw the boy wearin' a gun before today."

"Where the devil are them deputies of Rubeling's?" asked another.

"They won't show until Hatchet's out of town," Koney said sourly. "You can bet your bottom dollar on that."

"That Clem was as nice a boy as ever lived," muttered old Pruett. "Them Garriott buzzards, they sure get away with anythin', up to and includin' murder. This was murder, pure and simple. Young Clem never had a chance."

"They've gone too far this time," Koney said grimly. "Maybe the law won't get them, but Ash Cordell sure as Hades will!"

"This has been brewin' for years," Pruett said. "And this is just the beginnin'. There'll be a war now that'll tear the Carikaree from top to bottom!"

"Here comes them deputies, Paynter and Shokes," announced a voice.

"Yeah, right on schedule," said Koney with dry bitterness. "All them boys ever do is pick up the dead."

Chapter VIII

When Ash Cordell and Tannehill left Hillhouse that afternoon, they turned left out Western Avenue, clattered across the North Bridge over the Carikaree River, and followed the road in its northeasterly course along the Bittersweet. Their destination was the Double-D on Wagon Mound, but they had made no mention of the fact that they might be gone for three or four days. Ash didn't want to encourage Sue Ellen to see Gene Garriott again, or to let Clem know he had ample time to spend with Nita Dell.

Having started late, they spent that night in Chimney Rocks, a small ranching and farming community sheltered by a fantastic cluster of stone pillars and columns, from which the settlement derived its name. There were no Hatchet riders in town, but they learned that little Squeak Eakins and big Moose Blodwen had been there recently and gone on toward Wagon Mound. A few weeks previously Talboom had passed through with a Hatchet crew, bound for the same plateau. The Garriott men were keeping close tabs on some Wagon Mound outfit, but no open hostilities had been reported as yet.

Ash and Tan got an early start before daybreak in the morning, and were pushing toward the great tableland when the sun rose flaming from the Big Barrancas, far to the east. Ash Cordell was worried about the Delsing family ahead of them, and his own brother and sister back in Cadmus. He wished the two families were together in one spot; it would be a lot easier to watch over and protect them. Tannehill sang mournful cowboy dirges as they rode:

"Far away from his dear old Texas,
We laid him down to rest;
With his saddle for a pillow,
And his gun across his breast."

"You sure sing cheerful numbers, Tan," grumbled Cordell.

"Glad you like 'em, Cord," grinned Tannehill, and went on crooning in a low sad voice.

Leaving the Bittersweet for a cut-off, they crossed an arid section of sun-scorched rock and sand, creosote brush, catclaw and mesquite groves. Here and there blossomed clusters of spiny-wanded ocitollo and the spreading candelabra of saguaro cactus, thickets of mescal and bunches of cholla, stands of Spanish bayonet and bladed yucca. Emerging from this semi-desert of alkali flats and sandy dunes, they climbed to the vast broken surface of Wagon Mound in the furnace heat of afternoon, the riders sweat-soaked in the burning leather, their horses lather-frothed and wind-blown.

"This may be a short cut," drawled Tannehill, "but it sure cramps my singin' style, all this heat and dust."

"We'll come back on the Creek Road," Cordell comforted him, "so you can sing all the way, Tanny."

"That'll be fine, Cord. The miles are nothin' and time ceases to exist, when I am in good voice."

114

Along toward mid-afternoon, on Delsing land now, the flatted sound of wind-torn gunshots echoed from the walls of Scalplock Canyon before them. Slanting steeply up to the rimrock, their trained eyes quickly took in the situation. In the center of the open canyon floor, two riders were pinned down behind their dead horses, with two hidden riflemen sniping away at them from tumbled boulders on the rocky wall. Ash Cordell got out his field glasses and trained them on the pair that had been bushwhacked. As he had expected and feared, it was Dan Delsing and his son Fritz. He couldn't see enough of the sharp-shooters above to identify them, but it was a safe bet they were Hatchet riders, and probably Eakins and Blodwen.

Cordell handed the binoculars to Tannehill, and studied the landscape with his squinted gray eyes, that were taking on a green tinge at the promise of action ahead. The Delsings were alive and seemed to be unhurt thus far, but it would be only a matter of time before the marksmen above scored hits on them. Dan and Fritz were virtually helpless, pinned down so tightly they could scarcely get a shot off in return.

"I got a glimpse of a fat carcass up there that must belong to Blodwen," said Tannehill. "Which most likely means that his pardner is that withered-up little rat Eakins."

"That's what I figured, Tan. We'd better swing

around and come up on the rim behind them."

"Reckon so, Cord. It'll take a little time, but it's about the best way to get at 'em. Hope Dan and the kid keep their heads down and hang on."

"We hit Wagon Mound just about in time," Cordell said.

Tannehill smiled boyishly. "I'm beginnin' to believe what Rubeling said about you ridin' with trouble, Cord. On the other hand, it could be me that trouble loves."

"Or the other way around," grinned Cordell. "I never saw a long lean string of rawhide that loved trouble any more than one Tannehill."

Tan's brown eyes were dancing with yellowish lights. "I never shunned it, I reckon, any more than you did, Cordell."

They circled widely and climbed outer slopes of talus rock, the horses plowing strongly up drifts of gravel and shale, laboring steadily upward toward the outside rim. The grade was less precipitous than that of the inner wall, and they made good time on the blue roan and the mottled buckskin. Their estimate of angles and distances quite accurate, they reached the summit at a point almost directly above and behind the two riflemen from Hatchet. Ground-tying their sweat-rimmed mounts back in a clump of shrub cedar, they moved forward with their carbines and started working their way down the steep inside slope toward the enemy position.

It was slow painful going, with occasional dislodged pebbles threatening to start miniature avalanches that would give them away. The Hatchet rifles were hammering away with monotonous regularity to keep the Delsings nailed securely down on the canyon bottom. Now and then Dan or Fritz were able to fire back from their low barrier of horseflesh.

The ambushers had moved down since Cordell and Tannehill had first sighted them from afar, and were now about midway of the wall. Intervening brush and boulders obscured them, except for the smoke from their muzzles, but the two men above caught momentary glances of the Hatchet horses. Lowering themselves cautiously from handholds to footholds, utilizing all available cover and striving for silence, Cordell and Tannehill crept slowly down upon the enemy sharpshooters.

Then a tiny pebble slithered loose, gathering others and gaining momentum on the way, until a small landslide of earth and rocks was surging and smoking down the craggy wall. A hoarse shout of alarm went up, and bullets began droning up the slope toward Cordell and Tannehill, screeching off stone surfaces and raking up showers of dirt. Cordell slid into the shelter of a boulder. Tannehill, caught in the open, took a great flying leap downhill, lighting in a gravel drift with the dust billowing around him.

The massive bulk of Moose Blodwen came into view as the corpulent giant stood upright to line his sights on Tannehill, but the limber whiplike Tannehill rolled over and fired his carbine one-handed like a revolver before either Blodwen or Cordell could trigger. Blodwen grunted and lurched ponderously, his wild shot crackling harmlessly through the brush, and Cordell squeezed off with that huge bulk hung firmly on his front sight. The carbine slammed his shoulder, the high-powered report *spanging* clearly, and Moose Blodwen heaved over backward, thrashed for a few seconds in the brush, and was still. Tan and Ash both had bullets in him.

Little Squcak Eakins, a flitting warped form with tobacco swelling his wizened cheek, made a frenzied break for his horse, vaulted into the saddle, and went bucketing down a long shaly wash toward the canyon floor, the dust geysering high behind him. Tannehill and Cordell were on their feet, firing as fast as they could trigger and lever, but Eakins and his mount both seemed unhittable or impervious to lead.

Their carbines emptied, Cordell and Tannehill looked at each other in disgust, but the Delsings, father and son, were opening up on the Hatchet rider as he plunged wildly nearer the bottom of the gravel drift. The horse went down, cart-wheeling in a storm of dirt at the foot of the talus slope, flinging the small gunman clear with stunning force. Somehow Squeak Eakins clambered upright and staggered toward cover, but Dan and Fritz Delsing had him bracketed, dropping him before Eakins had taken three stumbling steps.

After making sure Blodwen was dead, Cordell waited with the giant's horse while Tannehill climbed the wall after their own mounts. Twisting up and lighting a cigarette, Cordell watched the Delsings remove their saddles and gear from the dead ponies and walk toward the bottom of the wall where Eakins had fallen. Tannehill returned, leading the sure-footed geldings, and they mounted up to ride wallowing down the sheer wash, Cordell trailing Blodwen's big brute behind him.

On the floor of the canyon, they dismounted and shook hands all around, the men grave and sober, but young Fritz elated and jubilant over his first battle.

"You boys pried us out of a mighty bad hole," Dan Delsing said, his square-jawed face solemn and powder-grimed. "They had us so we could hardly move a finger."

"You've been expectin' this, Dan?" asked Cordell.

Dan nodded his graying head. "They've been hangin' around watchin' us ever since you and Tan pulled out. Talboom was in a while back, with some Hatchet hides he claimed was found buried in my land. An old Garriott trick, of course. I knew then they'd be shootin' at us before long." He spat and smiled faintly. "Well, they couldn't have picked a better day for it."

"I knew it was you and Tan, Cord," said Fritz Delsing. "I told Dad so the minute we saw you up on the rim. Couldn't recognize you that far off, but I could feel it was you two."

"Anywhere there's powder burnin', you're apt to find us, Fritz," grinned Tannehill, drinking from his canteen and glancing at the bullet-torn body of Eakins. You and your dad did some pretty fair shootin', son."

"We heard you had a little run-in at Trelhaven," said Dan.

"There's goin' to be a lot of 'em from here on," Cordell said. "I just wish you folks weren't mixed up in it."

"Can't be helped, Cord," said Dan Delsing. "I wouldn't mind, if it wasn't for the family. Those Garriotts have got to be wiped out sometime, if the Carikaree's ever goin' to be a fit place to live in."

"You're goin' to stay, aren't you, Cord?" the boy said, turning his tow-head anxiously. "We had some riders, but they all got scared and hightailed off when they found out Hatchet was on us."

"Sure, Fritz, we'll be around," Cordell said. "Although there's a few things in Cadmus I may have to take care of, too."

"Let's get along home, boys," suggested Dan.

"Fritz and I can ride this big black, if you boys can pack our gear."

Cordell and Tannehill lashed the extra saddles and equipment onto their horses and stepped into leather, with Fritz riding behind his father on the black that had belonged to Blodwen. They had thrown Eakins' body out of sight in the brush. Cordell would have liked to bury both men and the dead Hatchet horse, but they didn't have the tools or the time.

"It'll be quite a few days, maybe a week or more, with luck," Cordell said thoughtfully, "before Hatchet finds out what happened to those two. By that time we should be able to get Rubeling out here with a posse. I think Tan and I better go back in tomorrow and start workin' on Rube."

"He said he'd throw in, if anybody hit the Delsings," remarked Tannehill.

Dan nodded. "Rube and I was always pretty good friends."

"How're Mrs. Delsing and Laura, Dan?" inquired Cordell.

"Some upset naturally, but fine otherwise. They'll sure be glad to see you two boys ridin' in."

"We aren't exactly sorry to hit the Double-D again," drawled Tannehill. "It's beginnin' to seem more like home than even the Hillhouse."

Dan Delsing slanted a questioning look, and Cordell inclined his head somberly. "Yes, my brother and sister grew up some while I was gone,

Dan. Natural, of course, but I guess I thought they never would."

"It jolts a man some, to find his young ones grown up all of a sudden," agreed Dan Delsing with understanding. "Fallin' in love, thinkin' of gettin' married—and fightin' gun battles."

Young Fritz laughed, his blue eyes sparkling. "I'm glad I got the first one under my belt, Dad," he said. "I always wondered if I could stand up to it like a man."

"You did, son, you sure did," said his father. "But I hope you never have to do it again, boy. You could stand bein' shot at again, Fritz, but I don't know as I could stand seein' it."

That evening after supper, Laura Delsing and Ash Cordell walked out behind the tool-shed and sat down in the grass with their backs to the board wall, watching the stars brighten in the darkening blue sky, and the moon come out white and luminous. They had discussed about everything that had occurred since their separation, and Cordell was rather quiet and thoughtful now, brooding on Sue Ellen and Clem with a strange chilling premonition of disaster, a cold sinking nausea in the pit of his stomach.

"Poor Ash," the girl murmured. "You had to go back to Cadmus, after all. And now this war is coming up. Everything's conspiring to keep you from doing what you want to do."

"It isn't that, Laura. I don't know what it is. I guess I'll never get to find that valley, and maybe it's just as well. I think we'd better get married this fall—after this trouble is over."

"Yes, Ash, that's what I want. If we're both still here, in the fall."

"We'll be here, Laura."

"I don't know, Ash. There's an awful feeling inside me. Shouldn't we get married now, before it starts?"

"No, that wouldn't be right. And there isn't time, Laura."

"It would be better than nothing."

"Don't talk that way, Laura," he said. "We're goin' to have everythin', all the rest of our lives together."

Cordell held her in the strong circle of his arm, and looked at the sculptured loveliness of the face resting on his shoulder, the long-lashed mystery of the eyes, the saucy tilted nose and broad gracious mouth, the perfect purity of the serene brow and curved cheekbones. The clean line of the jaws and chin, the flawless beauty of the tanned throat. He inhaled the fragrance of her soft curling hair, and bent his head until his lips rested on the sweet fullness of hers, gently at first and then with increasing pressure. Her mouth responded in kind, urgent and deliciously afire, and her arms gripped him hard. The wonder and rapture filled them as before.

But that cold blade of fear turned once more, deep and low inside Cordell, cooling and slowing the torrent of his blood. He let go of her, half turning away, and a low cry came from him. It was no good; it wouldn't be good, free and unrestrained, until the war with the Garriotts was over and the Carikaree was at peace.

After a few minutes, Cordell rose and lifted Laura to her feet with lithe ease. They kissed once more, lightly and tenderly this time, and turned to walk back through shadow-patterned moonlight toward the lighted windows of the ranch house.

"Tan and I better turn in," Cordell said. "We want to get an early start tomorrow. There's no telling when Hatchet will learn about those two men. I want to get Rubeling organized before Hatchet can strike."

"Yes, I know, I know," Laura Delsing murmured, infinitely wise and weary and sorrowful. "Love always comes last, in this country. Men and guns come first. . . ." She broke off, sobbing softly, and then her voice went up fiercely. "I hate it, I hate it! All this fighting and suffering and killing, Ash. What good does it do, what sense is there in it? Oh, this mad, bloody, hate-ridden country! My own little brother, shooting and killing at seventeen!"

"It's bad, Laura; we know it's bad," Cordell said, trying to comfort her with his arms. "But the Garriotts are worse. Men have to fight for their rights, or go under, Laura. The Garriotts have run wild long enough. There'll never be peace in this valley until Hatchet is put down."

"You're right, Ash," she whispered brokenly. "Of course you're right. But I still hate it with everything in me!"

"Sometimes I hate it too, Laura," said Ash Cordell. "Tonight is one of them. But we've got to fight; there's no other way. And you'll fight with us, if you have to, Laura."

"Sure, I'll fight." She laughed rather harshly, wildly. "I can shoot as well as Fritz. If he can kill, I can kill too!"

"We'll hope neither of you have to," Cordell said. "There are enough of us who were made for that, I reckon."

"I'm sorry, Ash. I didn't mean to go to pieces. I'm not really as flighty and finicky as that, darling."

"You're all right, Laura. You're the finest loveliest girl in the world."

She smiled bravely up at him. "That's taking in a lot of territory, Mister Cordell. But I will make you a mighty fine wife—when all the shooting's over."

The following afternoon when Cordell and Tannehill rode into Chimney Rocks, looking forward to a drink and a break there, Tan was singing in a plaintive lilting voice:

125

"All night long we trailed him,
Through mesquite and chaparral;
And I had to think of that woman,
As I saw him pitch and fall."

They were standing at the bar in the Lucky Seven Saloon when a dust-covered rider came in and started talking about some shooting in Cadmus Flats. The customers and idlers clustered eagerly about him for the details. Cordell, deep in morbid thought, was paying little attention until he saw a look of disbelief and then horror on Tannehill's lean leathery face. A terrible fear filled Cordell as he wheeled away from the bar; some of the men were already shushing the speaker with words and motions.

"What was that you were sayin'?" asked Cordell clearly, walking toward the group, the men shrinking back before him.

"Gawd Almighty!" groaned the dusty messenger. "I didn't see you, Cord. I don't like to bring you this kinda news, Cord."

"Who was killed?" Cordell demanded relentlessly, knowing the answer even as he asked the question.

"Cord, I'm sorry. Your brother Clem. Day before yesterday."

Cordell's fingers were biting deep into the man's arms. "You know that, for sure?"

He gulped and nodded, wilting in that steel

grasp. "Kyler Garriott killed him, out front of the Longhorn. Shot him three times."

"Where's Kyler?"

"He rode out with Hamrick and Laidlaw. Nobody's seen 'em since."

"What's Rubeling doin'?"

"Waitin' for you, Cord, I guess."

For the first time Cordell seemed to realize that he was gripping the man's arms with crushing, paralyzing force. "Sorry," he said. "Didn't mean to—And thanks, thanks for tellin' me." Cordell turned to Tannehill. "Come on, Tan; let's ride."

Tannehill threw money on the bar and said: "Give me a bottle to take along. I reckon we'll be needin' it." Carrying the bottle in his hand, Tannehill followed Cordell out through the batwings into the blinding glare of the street. Without a word they unwrapped their reins from the bleached worn rail, swung into the sun-warmed leather, and rode out the single street of Chimney Rocks toward the Carikaree and Cadmus.

Chapter IX

The office in the Big House at Hatchet was much as Cordell had remembered it, more like a luxurious library or drawing room than an office. Gurney Garriott enjoyed rich living and opulent surroundings. Cordell and Tannehill, feeling undressed without their gun-belts, paced the large high-ceilinged room while awaiting old Gurney. Outside, Sheriff Rubeling and his deputies were making a cursory token search for Kyler, although Rube felt certain Gurney was telling the truth when he said Kyler was not on the ranch. Old Gurney had not welcomed the intrusion of the law, and his look at Rubeling indicated that Rube would never see another term in office.

"How long has it been murder in this country, when two men stand up and shoot it out?" demanded Gurney, adding: "In broad daylight, on the main street of a town."

"I'm not makin' any official charge yet, Gurney," said Rubeling. "I'd just like to talk with Kyler."

"So would I!" snapped Gurney. "But darned if I know where he's at."

This was the first real opportunity Cordell had been given to inspect the headquarters of Gurney Garriott, and he was making the most of it. The hardwood floor was covered with thick carpets, soft under their boots, and the paneled walls were lined with bookshelves, hung with oil paintings and portraits, fitted with full-length mirrors. A great flat-topped oak desk gleamed with a dull rich luster, and behind it were filing cases and a tall carved cabinet filled with glittering bottles of expensive liquor. There were racks of rifles and revolvers, a broad fieldstone fireplace, leather easy chairs and couches. Crystal chandeliers were suspended in shimmering brilliance from the lofty paneled ceiling. Cordell and Tannehill felt rather uneasy in such an elegant setting.

Ash was scanning the family portraits when old Gurney returned. The subject of one had obviously been Gurney's father, regal and overbearing, proud, rock-jawed and aquiline-nosed. The man in the next frame resembled someone Cordell had known or seen, and then he realized with a shock that the remembered likeness was what he saw on the rare occasions when he studied himself in a mirror. It gave him an eerie, awed feeling to discover almost his own image on the wall of this Garriott chamber.

"Who was that, Gurney?" he asked, pointing out the portrait.

"An uncle, my father's brother," Gurney said, looking from the picture to Cordell and back again. "That's strange, Ash. You look a little like that uncle of mine, as you grow older."

"Black sheep, I suppose?" Cordell murmured.

"Well, not exactly. He had his good points, as well as bad." Gurney settled ponderously behind the desk, and motioned them into chairs before it. "I've been expecting you, Ash," he said, sighing. "Didn't expect a sheriff's posse, but that's all right. I was sorry to hear what happened in town, Ash, sorrier than I can put into words. It was almost like one brother killing another. I don't know, Ash." He made a weary gesture. "I tried to do the best I could for all of you. But you always hated us, Ash. I thought Clem was different, but perhaps he hated us, too."

"Why did you take us in that way?"

Gurney mulled that over a moment. "I saw a chance to do something good and decent. My motives were partly selfish, I'll admit. I knew how people were talking about Hatchet. I thought a kind generous act might make them see us in a better light. Wrong, of course. I was just heaping coals of fire on my own head, as it turned out. But I meant well, Ash; I meant well by you children."

"You did all right by us, Gurney," said Cordell. "But I still feel that you know something about our folks, and how they happened to be killed up there in the mountains."

"Nothing whatever, Ash, as I've told you a hundred times."

Gurney Garriott was a giant of a man, going

slowly overweight and fat, but with an iron hardness underlying the massive flesh. His character was evident in the bold heavy thrust of the jaws, the large arrogant Roman nose, piercing black eyes under shaggy brows, and the domineering set of his big head with its thick mane of iron-gray hair. Here was a man who had built up a dynasty for himself, and he had all the essential qualities of the conqueror: ruthless power, shrewd fore-sight, vast confidence, a remorseless willful drive, single-minded purpose, and boundless ambition. Sitting back, solid and comfortable in his oak and leather chair, he surveyed his two visitors with cool tolerant interest.

"You don't know where Kyler's gone?" Cordell asked flatly.

"I haven't the slightest idea, Ash."

"Where's Gene?"

"I don't know that either. But Gene had nothing to do with it. Gene's a good boy, without any of the wild bad streak that's in Kyler and in you, Ash."

"I'll find Kyler," said Cordell simply.

"You won't rest until Kyler's dead or you are dead?"

"That's right, Gurney. That's the way it is now."

Old Gurney Garriott shook his kingly head. "It was a fair fight, Ash. You've killed men over nothing more important than a dance hall girl.

You killed Thorner over that same girl, in Trelhaven."

"That was different," Cordell said. "This was plain murder. Kyler's always been a gunman and killer. Clem never used a gun in his life."

"He was wearing one."

"Sure, Kyler prodded him into that."

Gurney sighed heavily. "I can see that you're set, Ash. Nothing will change you or stop you but a bullet."

Ash Cordell nodded, the bones of his cheeks and jaws standing out sharper than ever under the bronzed skin, his wide mouth thinned straight and hard, his gray eyes flaring with green fire. "Are you plannin' to move against the Delsings on Wagon Mound?" he asked.

"Why, no," Gurney said. "What makes you ask that, Ash?"

"Don't do it, Gurney," advised Cordell quietly. "If you do, Hatchet will come right down on your head."

Gurney Garriott chortled deep in his throat. "I could have you killed right here. You know that, Ash."

"It wouldn't be very smart, Gurney. That's one murder you'd get charged with. You think Rubeling's your man, but he isn't any more. He's been some scared of you but he's gettin' over it. Rube thought a lot of Clem, and so did everybody else in Cadmus."

"You're the smart one, Ash. To come here with Rubeling, and without your guns. You don't want to die, do you, Ash?" Gurney was suavely taunting now.

Cordell smiled gravely. "There's a few things I'd like to do first."

"I won't set anyone on you, Ash. Unless it's to save Kyler."

"Nothing'll save Kyler," stated Cordell.

"You aren't going after Gene too, are you, boy?"

"Not if he keeps away from my sister."

Gurney shook his noble gray head. "You're hard, Ash, hard and cold as steel. Too bad you never applied yourself to anything worthwhile. You might have amounted to something, boy."

"Like you?" Cordell laughed in soft mockery. "No, thanks, Gurney. Come on, Tan; we're wastin' our time here. Maybe we can get out of here this once without gettin' shot up."

"You won't be coming back, Ash." It was not a question.

"Not until I hear Kyler is hidin' out here."

"Do you think *you'd* hear it, if he was?"

"I do," Cordell said firmly. "There are men here who don't love you or your sons, Gurney."

"Get out!" Gurney roared suddenly, showing anger for the first time, sledging a huge fist down on the gleaming desktop. "Get out while you can!"

Ash Cordell grinned. "Still got some of that temper left, I see."

Outside in the yard dusk was settling, and Hatchet was at supper. A muted clatter and hum came from the long dining hall and cook shack. The ranch was larger, more like a complete community than ever, with additional buildings and lamps glowing along the company streets. Hatchet housed an army of riders, thought Cordell, and it would take another army to wipe the place out. Waiting out near the gate, Rubeling and his three deputies looked small, lost and helpless, pathetic and insignificant.

A lone rider with enormous broad shoulders and a strangely squat body sat waiting in the saddle where their horses were tethered. This man's face was wide and grotesquely ugly like his bulk, Cordell observed as they walked closer to the hitch-rail, the features conveying the same impression of deformity that the powerful hunched body did. It was a froglike face with dark mottled skin, full and fleshy with a thick flattened nose. Wide down-turned lips bulged over protruding teeth, and the hooded eyes shone like an animal's in the gloomy light.

The creature was silent while they mounted. Cordell felt his scalp crawl under his hat, and cold stirred icily in the pit of his stomach.

"I'm Hodkey," the man said, in a deep rough voice. "Just a mite curious, is all. Cordell, you'd look a whole lot better with a gun-belt on."

"I'll wear it for you next time," promised Ash easily, but chills were prickling up his spine into the back of his neck.

Hodkey made a weird chuckling sound in his throat. "Right obligin' of you, sonny. I reckon you boys know who I am?"

"You said your name was Hodkey," drawled Tannehill.

Hodkey looked straight at Tannehill. "That don't mean nothin' to you, huh?" He laughed, a gibbering and hideous sound in the dusk. "Well, I just wanted a good look at you boys. I like to know my men, alive or dead, and no mistakes. I'll know you the next time." Hodkey saluted insolently, pulled his horse about, and cantered away.

"That character don't need a gun," Tannehill said, as they loped out toward the gate. "His face'll do the job."

"So that's Hodkey?" mused Ash Cordell. "The man everybody hears about and nobody ever sees. His brag is that he's killed more men than cholera and smallpox, they say. I reckon we're next on his list, Tanny."

Hodkey meanwhile had pulled up in front of the doorway, in which old Gurney Garriott was standing. "A mistake, lettin' them go, Gurney."

"They were unarmed, Hod. They had the sheriff with them. What are you going to do?"

"Kill them," Hodkey said. "Kill the sheriff and his deputies too."

"Times are changing, Hod," said Gurney. "Public opinion's turning against us more than ever. Kyler made the mistake when he shot young Clem Cordell."

"Who's goin' to hurt us?" demanded Hodkey. "We can sweep the Carikaree clean from the Barrancas to the Madrelinos, if we have to."

"It's a good thing I keep you out of this valley and up in the mountains, Hod," said Gurney Garriott with a wry smile. "Your ideas are outdated."

Hoofs clopped through the growing darkness, and a column of riders filed in from the northwest, the body of them halting at one of the stables, a single horseman coming on toward the Big House. It was Talboom, high and lanky in the saddle, his knobby beaked face harsh with anger.

"We found Eakins and Blodwen, or what the vultures had left of 'em," Talboom reported. "In Scalplock Canyon on Wagon Mound. They downed two Double-D horses, but missed the men. Somebody came up and jumped Moose and Squeak from behind, it looked like. Anyway they're dead and picked pretty clean."

"What did you do about the Delsings, Tal?" asked Gurney.

"Not much, waitin' on orders from you, Gurney.

136

I gave them forty-eight hours to clear out, but I doubt if they'll move."

"All right, we'll move them," Gurney Garriott said. "Hodkey, here's a chance to work off some of that bloodlust of yours. Pick a crew and ride for Wagon Mound tonight. You know what to do when you get there. Burn out Double-D, round up every head of stock on the place, and drive for the hills. Make it fast before any posse can get out from Cadmus."

"You think they'll send a posse after *us?*" Hodkey asked incredulously.

"They will this time," Gurney said grimly. "I told you times were changing in the Carikaree."

Cordell and Tannehill, in the meantime, had joined Sheriff Rubeling's party of Deputies Shokes, Maddern and Paynter, and they were heading westward along the river toward Blue Butte and Cadmus Flats. In response to Rubeling's first questioning look, Cordell had spread his palms emptily.

"I don't think Kyler's there," the sheriff said. "They've got a Hatchet hideout somewhere in the mountains. Hodkey stays there most of the time. Kyler probably lined out for that, along with Red and Pretty Boy."

"That was Hodkey we met in there," drawled Tannehill. "Worth the trip."

"Hodkey!" cried Maddern. "Was that Hodkey? I thought there was somethin' familiar about that

rider waitin' for you boys. I was in Abilene the day Hodkey killed three of them Possehls. I never saw anythin' like that Hodkey with the six-guns. One Possehl never got his iron out. The other two fired, but they was dead when their guns went off, one up in the air, the other almost blowin' his own foot off."

"Hodkey's face probably paralyzed them," Tannehill said.

"It's enough to paralyze a rattlesnake," said Maddern. "Hickok was town marshal of Abilene then, Wild Bill himself, but he never tried to take Hodkey."

"What do you figure on doin', Ash?" inquired Rubeling.

"Hatchet's goin' to be ridin' against the Delsings," said Cordell. "We've got to get a posse out there, Rube, if we can raise one."

"We'll try, Ash, as soon as we can get back tomorrow night. But there aren't too many men in Cadmus who want to buck the Garriotts, right out in the open. You know that as well as I do."

"I know, Rube. We'll just have to do the best we can."

"Maybe round up ten or a dozen," Rubeling predicted. "Nowhere near enough but I wouldn't gamble on gettin' any more than that."

"We'll go along with what we can get," Cordell said.

"It's a sad state of affairs," Tannehill drawled,

"when there's only ten or twelve men with any guts in a town as big as Cadmus Flats."

"Livin' in towns, gettin' married, and raisin' families, it does somethin' to men," said Rubeling, tall, brooding and hawklike on his spirited roan. "Maybe somethin'll wake 'em up—sometime."

The next night they crossed the East Bridge over the Carikaree and rode in past the familiar lighted places of Front Street. Music was tinkling from the Rio Belle, *Moonlight on the Hudson*, and Ash Cordell thought bitterly of Nita Dell and his brother Clem, dead and buried at twenty-five, before he had even started living. The death of one man was a trivial thing in the scheme of things, and the world went on as if nothing had happened, as if that man never had existed. It was terrible to think that the death of a man, your own brother, could cause such a small fleeting stir in the pattern of events. It made all life seem futile, empty and inconsequential. A man's passing was little more than the dropping of a pebble into a pool of water. The ripples spread, faded, and were forgotten. It filled Cordell with resentful fury and hatred that life and death could be so meaningless; humanity so callous and indifferent.

Racking their horses in front of the Longhorn Saloon, close by the spot on the sandy boardwalk where Clement Cordell had died, the six riders shouldered through the slatted doors and lined

139

up at the bar. Koney, setting out the bottle and glasses, paused before Cordell.

"Young fellah in here lookin' for you, Ash. Name of Bob Woodlee."

Cordell sighed deeply. "More trouble, I reckon."

"Why, I don't know; he didn't act hostile. Seemed right friendly, Ash, and all cut up when he heard about Clem. Wasn't he the Woodlee boy whose folks got killed up on the Bittersweet, five–six years back?"

"That's him, Koney."

"Reckon he's waitin' up at the Hillhouse," said Koney. "Allowed he was real anxious to see you. Just in from Wagon Mound and had somethin' important to tell you and Tan."

"Thanks, Koney. We'll get along home and see him right away."

Koney's thin acidulous face creased with one of his rare crooked smiles. "Look at me!" he muttered. "Drivin' business away from my own bar. No wonder I don't get rich like other saloon-keepers."

Cordell and Tannehill drank up, said good night to the sheriff, deputies and others, and departed. Rubeling followed them outside and promised to drum up a posse ready to ride in the morning. The other two mounted and swung along the street toward the Hillhouse Hotel, looming on its elevated bench at the west end. Leaving their horses with the hostler in the stable, with instructions for a good rubdown and graining, Ash and Tan walked stiffly back to the kitchen entrance on long saddle-cramped legs.

Ma Muller was sitting bowed over the table, her gray head on her arms, her shoulders tremulous with silent sobbing. Bob Woodlee sat opposite her, a glass of whisky in his hand, a look of unhappiness on his plain, pleasant brown face. Woodlee rose and shook hands with them firm and hard without speaking.

Cordell laid his arm around the woman's hunched shoulders. "Come on, Ma. Aren't you even goin' to say hello? This is no good, Ma; you've got to cut it out." Ma Muller raised her tear-stained face slowly, looking up at Cordell with blurred stricken blue eyes, shaking her head in abject desolation. Clem's death had hit her hard, aging her years in the past few days, and now there was something else.

"Your sister's gone, Ash boy," she said, her voice strained and shaken. "Sue Ellen's gone! Gone without sayin' a word or leavin' a message or anythin'. That's not like Sue Ellen, not at all, Ash. Somebody must've taken her off. Maybe you were right about Gene Garriott, after all."

"Gene wouldn't hurt her, Ma," said Cordell, "or take her away if she wasn't willing to go. She must have gone of her own accord, Ma, and I suppose I drove her to it. The worst that'll happen to Sue Ellen is that she'll marry a

Garriott, Ma, and I guess that's what she wants." Ash was sorely hurt and troubled by this news, but he could not reveal it when Ma needed cheering and comforting.

Ma Muller did derive some satisfaction from his words and his presence. "Perhaps you're right, Ash; they might have eloped. Anyway, I can't be mopin' around and carryin' on like this. Let me fix you boys somethin' nice to eat now."

They all protested that they had eaten, and insisted that she go to bed and try to get some sleep and rest. After Ma Muller had retired, Bob Woodlee said:

"First I've got to apologize for makin' a downright fool of myself in Trelhaven, boys. I've been ashamed ever since. You had that girl tagged right, and I was all wrong."

"Forget it, Woody," Cordell told him. "It's over and done with."

"I'd like to kill Nita Dell myself," Woodlee went on bitterly. "After hearin' what she did to Clem, I could blast her with pleasure!"

"What about Wagon Mound, Woody?"

"Hatchet riders found the two dead men in Scalplock Canyon, and gave the Delsings forty-eight hours to get out. I took Mrs. Delsing and Laura to Chimney Rocks, but they wouldn't come any farther. Dan and the boy stayed on the ranch; nothing could make them leave."

Ash Cordell swore softly. "We were takin' a

posse up there tomorrow, Woody. But I reckon we'd better start tonight, if we can round up anybody at all. Or even if we can't."

"Yes, the sooner the better," Woodlee said. "Hatchet may be on the march already."

"So we saddle up again," grinned Tannehill. "Seems like we been straddlin' leather ever since I can remember, night and day. Better pack all the grub we can, Cord. This is liable to be a long rough one."

"A good thing we didn't take our own horses to Hatchet," said Cordell. "Blue and Bucky are all rested up for us. Woody, you'll be needin' a fresh mount too. We've got a chestnut mare for you out back. I'll leave a note for Ma—and borrow some of her whiskey."

"I hope I catch up with Hamrick and Laidlaw somewhere along," Bob Woodlee said. "I know them two and Kyler Garriott were in that raid on our place, on the Bittersweet, and I know Ash wants Kyler. Laidlaw, just a kid like me then, tied me to that wagon wheel, and Hamrick cut me to pieces with a bullwhip. Never told anybody this before."

Cordell and Tannehill nodded solemnly. They had seen the wicked scars that striped Woodlee's back, from his neck to the base of his spine.

Chapter X

At the start there had been great interest and excitement in Cadmus, and it looked as if they were going to have a large posse riding that night. Until Rubeling said: "It may mean ridin' against Hatchet, you men might as well know now." That cooled down most of the loafers, and sobered off most of the drunks.

It also caused little Koney to shuck off his apron in the Longhorn, buckle on his gun, and start for the Riverside Corral after his horse. And it brought old Pruett, the saddlemaker, out of his shop carrying an old Sharps .50, and calling on Koney to fetch back his horse too. There were others who really wanted to go, but were held back by various reasons, domestic, business and professional, or general unpreparedness. These pledged to follow up with another posse.

There were only ten riders in the group that left the Flats at 1:08 that summer morning, clomping across North Bridge and heading up the Creek Road alongside of the Bittersweet. Ash Cordell, Tannehill and Bob Woodlee. Sheriff Rubeling with four deputies, Maddern, Shokes, Paynter and Chesbro. The small sour-faced balding Koney, and the ancient gray-mustached Pruett. They weren't nearly strong enough for a head-on showdown fight, for there was certain to be a score or more of Garriott hands on the Wagon Mound expedition. But they might be in time to save Dan Delsing and his son Fritz.

They reached Chimney Rocks not long after sun-up, and learned with dismay that Mrs. Delsing and Laura had ridden back to the Double-D. A man came out of the Lucky Seven Saloon, the man who had brought the news of Clem's death to the Rocks that day, introducing himself as Andruss, Andy for short, and saying he'd like to join them. He was made welcome and the column moved on into the north, toward the vast natural terrace of Wagon Mound with the Shellerdines shouldering up in jagged splendor against the distant northern horizon. The already grim men were bleaker than ever, fearful that the two Delsing women had returned to a certain and sudden death with the men of the family.

They pushed on as fast as possible, without punishing their mounts too severely in the fierce heat, but to Ash Cordell the pace seemed agonizingly and maddeningly slow. It was agreed to follow Bittersweet Creek all the way this trip, to spare horses and riders the sun-blasted desert crossing of the short cut. Wagon Mound was looming close in the afternoon glare when the crackle of distant gunfire came to them. Cordell groaned aloud, "Too late, too late," and others cursed or prayed silently, according to their nature, wagging sun-dazed heads and gnawing parched lips.

"I'm goin' on ahead, Rube," said Cordell.

"Don't do anythin' rash now," Rubeling warned. "Don't charge the whole Hatchet outfit, Ash. Throwin' your own life away won't help the Delsings or anybody else."

Cordell lifted his blue roan out in front of the posse. Tannehill and Woodlee promptly put their horses after him, and the trio soon left the main force behind. The firing rolled up louder and steadier as they climbed to the surface of Wagon Mound, until it sounded like a full-scale battle on the interior. Driving on along the high bank of the Bittersweet, they checked their weapons as they rode, all three of them having strapped on double-holstered belts and extra guns for this campaign.

"Two men against twenty or thirty," moaned Cordell. "Dan and the kid are doin' well to hold out this long. I hope it started before Mom and Laura could get back there."

The sounds of battle rose and fell on the molten air, rumbling and muttering like a distant summer thunderstorm. The banks of the creek were lower as they progressed into the plateau, and far ahead they could see the faint line of the irrigation ditch that diverged eastward toward the

Double-D. After a walking rest, they threw the horses into a run, while the rifle fire swelled in volume and intensity, and Cordell felt like screaming out in rage against the cruelty of the time and space that left them so helpless. The racketing guns died out as they neared the ditch, and then Cordell saw two horses in a clump of cottonwoods, empty-saddled, and two feminine figures huddled nearby on the shady ground.

For a horrible moment he thought they were lifeless, and then he saw Laura moving, apparently trying to soothe and comfort her mother. Kicking the slate-colored gelding into a gallop, Cordell raced toward those trees, Tan and Woody pounding after him. The firing had ceased entirely by the time they drew up under the cottonwoods and flung themselves from the leather. That meant it was all over at the ranch; Dan and Fritz were dead or dying. Almost immediately smoke started billowing up gray-black into the sunlight about the Double-D. The three men tried to screen the sight from Laura and her mother.

The Delsing women were unhurt, although Mom was nearly in a state of collapse from grief and despair. Laura's fine carved features were shining with sweat, streaked with powder and dirt, as she lifted her bright chestnut head.

"They drove us away, Ash," she said hollowly. "We couldn't get anywhere near the place. They started shooting at us, but I don't think they tried to hit us. There must be thirty or more of them."

"The shooting's stopped!" Mrs. Delsing cried, jerking up from her reclining position. "And look! The place is burning! Dear God in Heaven—" She broke off, sobbing.

"You stay here, Laura," said Cordell. "We'll go along and see."

"No!" Mrs. Delsing was scrambling to her feet. "We're going with you. It's our men in there!"

"Better stay back," Cordell said gently, swinging aboard his blue roan, Tannehill and Woodlee following suit. Wheeling out of the trees, they hurtled toward the irrigation ditch and the smoke clouds towering beyond that hill shoulder. Glancing back once, Cordell saw that the Delsing women had mounted and were coming after them.

Clearing the sloping flank of the hill at last, they came in sight of the burning ranch buildings. Hatchet had pulled out, its murderous task accomplished, a saffron haze in the east marking the course of retreat. Every structure on Double-D had been oil-soaked and fired, flaring up hot and bright, the smoke columns rising dense and high, merging overhead to darken the sunlit sky. The smell of the smoke made Cordell sick with old cruel memories, and Bob Woodlee's face paled and drew bone-tight under the tan.

Peering through slitted eyes they rode forward, taut dry lips snarling back on their teeth, rage and hate and a need for violence boiling up

148

within them. The horses snorted and shied; as the heat reached out toward them in scorching, shimmering waves, the evil stench choking man and beast alike. There were dead horses on the plain but no human bodies visible, and no signs of life anywhere.

"In there, you reckon?" muttered Tannehill, nodding toward the blackening charred shell of the ranch house. Flame and smoke erupted from it in swirling pillars of gray, brown and black, laced with scarlet and gold. Piling up and spreading aloft, the billowing mass formed false thunder-heads that shut out the sun.

Bob Woodlee sniffed the air and shook his head. "Nobody in there, boys. I know the smell."

"Where the devil, then?" Tan's amber eyes probed the conflagration.

"There's Dan!" said Cordell, jumping down and dropping his reins, running with the stiff awkward grace of a rider toward the irrigation ditch, the other two vaulting clear and legging it after him.

Dan Delsing lay spread-eagled on the wall of the ditch, only his head and shoulders showing, his square powder-blackened face bowed across the carbine. As tenderly as possible, they hauled him up over the edge and laid him out on the bleached yellow grass. Delsing had been shot in the left shoulder and right leg, but not fatally nor even seriously, Cordell concluded. In both cases the slugs had gone right through. Dan opened his eyes as Cordell bathed the wounds.

"Fritz?" he panted. "Out by—the corrals. He went down—out there. Dead, I guess—the boy's dead."

"Maybe not, Dan," said Cordell. "We'll see in a minute. You're goin' to be all right, Dan."

Delsing gestured weakly, as if to say that was irrelevant. Laura and her mother rode up and dismounted then, and Mrs. Delsing knelt quickly beside her husband. "I'll take care of Dan, Ash," she said. "You go find Fritz."

Cordell rose and looked at Laura. "Help your mother," he said. "We'll be right back."

They circled the blazing bonfires of the ranch yard and found young Fritz stretched face down in the dirt by the corral rails, his straw-colored head bright in the sunshine. There was an old Walker Colt in his left hand, a Henry rifle in the right. He looked shot to pieces, his shirt and pants drenched with blood, but he opened his glazed blue eyes when Cordell lifted and turned him over with gentle care.

"Dad—all right?"

"Sure, he's fine, Fritz."

The childish grimed face tried to smile. "Heck of a fight, Ash. Too bad you missed it."

"We'll catch up with 'em," Cordell promised.

"We got some of 'em," Fritz panted agonizingly. "But they was too many."

"You sure gave 'em a fight, you and Dan," said

150

Cordell, trying to keep his voice from catching and breaking. "You'll do to take along, pardner."

Fritz Delsing smiled faintly, proudly, and started coughing. That brought a bright crimson gush from his boyish lips, and when it was over the blue eyes were sightless, the young life gone. Ash Cordell laid him easily back on the earth and stood up, blinking his eyes rapidly, looking at the somber sunburned faces around him. Rubeling and the rest of his men had come up now.

"Seventeen years old," Cordell said. "From here on every Garriott, every Hatchet man I see, is dead!"

"Dan isn't hit bad," Rubeling said, his hawk-face fierce and gaunt. "I'm sendin' Chesbro back to bring up a big posse. He'll have a wagon sent out from Chimney Rocks to pick up Dan and the women. We'd better keep on the trail."

"They won't be hard to follow," someone said. "They're drivin' all the stock they can pick up on the run."

"Dan say who was in the bunch, Rube?" asked Cordell.

"Hodkey and Talboom, for sure. And he thought he saw Kyler Garriott with Hamrick and Laidlaw."

"That's good," Cordell said.

"Looks like they headed back to Hatchet," said Tannehill. "Or all the way into the Big Barrancas." Andruss, the Chimney Rocks rider, spoke then, rather surprisingly: "No, boys. They've got a place up in the Shellerdines, where they hold their rustled cattle. They'll hit for there, I reckon."

"You know where it is, Andruss?" asked Rubeling.

"Not exactly, but I got a notion," Andruss said. "They'll lead us to it anyhow."

"Well, let's roll," Rubeling said. "Hate to leave the Delsings, but there's nothin' we can do here."

"Tan and I better stay a little while," Ash Cordell said, looking down at the dead boy beside the corral. "We'll catch up in a couple of hours, Rube."

"Sure, you do that, Ash," said the sheriff. "We'll be seein' you."

The posse went on eastward across Wagon Mound toward the Spires, on the trail of the Hatchet raiders and their stolen herd. Cordell and Tannehill turned back to the fiery wreckage of the Double-D, where the flames chewed briskly and the smoke mushroomed high, black and evil in the sunny afternoon. Cottonwoods were exploding in the heat.

The three surviving Delsings waited on the other side of the burning buildings. At this moment, with Fritz dead, thought Cordell, it would be a lot easier to go against all the hordes of Hatchet than it was to face this grief-stricken mother, father and sister.

Ash Cordell had known the urge to kill before, but never as strong and savage as he felt it now.

First his brother Clem, now young Fritz, and Sue Ellen gone with Gene Garriott. Yes, and he was sure now that the Garriotts had somehow been responsible for the murder of his father and mother. That had been in the Hatchet tradition, with guns and torches.

With the fire reek in their nostrils, Cordell and Tannehill walked back toward where Laura and Mom Delsing were sitting beside the wounded Dan, gazing at the smoldering destruction of their home.

"I knew the boy was dead," Dan Delsing said. "I wouldn't have hit for the ditch if I hadn't seen Fritz go down. We dropped four–five of them, Ash; they must've lugged 'em off. Quite a kid, that Fritz. I couldn't ask for a better man to side me. Mom, Laura, don't cry so, girls. It was meant to be, we've got to figure it that way. We'll bury him right here, because we'll be buildin' here again, and we want him with us.

"I've got a feelin'," Dan went on. "Double-D's goin' to be here long after the Garriotts have gone under."

They buried Fritz on the slope over the smoke-shrouded ranch site, Cordell and Tannehill digging the grave deep, filling it and securing it with stones piled as markers. Leaving a bottle of Ma Muller's whiskey with Dan Delsing, they mounted and followed their lengthening distorted shadows east in the waning afternoon.

Chapter XI

Cordell and Tannehill overtook the posse before nightfall near the eastern perimeter of Wagon Mound, and they made a cold camp within view of the Hatchet fires on the prairie between the plateau and the Spires. The Garriott forces, driving a few hundred head of cattle, left a trail as broad and plain as a thoroughfare to follow, and the sheriff's party had to slow down to stay behind them. Hatchet, overconfident in its power and disdainful of any possible pursuit, could have been overhauled and taken, had Rubeling's been a larger company. But ten riders were not enough to throw against thirty or more.

The following day, as Andruss had predicted, the rustlers turned north from the Spires and headed into the foothills of the Shellerdine Mountains. Somewhere in the highlands, according to Andruss, they had a hidden valley, presided over by Hodkey, where stolen herds were pastured until Hatchet altered the brands and fleshmarks and disposed of them. Ash Cordell began to wonder if this Garriott hideout and his long-sought Cathedral Valley could be one and the same. He and Tan had combed the Shellerdines, but a lifetime wasn't long enough to cover the entire mountain wilder-ness. They could easily have missed it in their earlier explorations.

Excitement gripped Cordell as they mounted higher into the range that third day, and he saw landscapes that were like something dimly remembered from a dream, scenes that were vaguely but hauntingly familiar, places he was certain he had looked upon in some previous life. This had happened before in his wide roving excursions, but never had it impressed him so deeply. At various levels, they came upon holding grounds where cattle had been grazed and bedded over a period of years, which substantiated Andruss' story.

"Funny we never hit these cow trails and bed grounds up here, Tan," mused Cordell.

"Seems odd now," Tannehill said. "But the Shellerdines are mighty big, Cord, and they run for hundreds of miles."

For a long time that night Cordell was unable to sleep in the mountain coldness, lying awake in his blankets, backed against the softly snoring Tannehill for warmth, thinking endless and troubled thoughts of many things. He saw himself at ten, crouched on that ladder under the trapdoor, hearing the gunshots that had killed his mother and father, seeing those booted legs tramp to and fro, and that one ugly built-up boot he had been searching for ever since. Seventeen years ago, or more now, about the time Fritz Delsing was born.

He saw Clem sprawled dead on the street in Cadmus Flats, Sue Ellen laughing happily in the arms of Gene Garriott, and Ma Muller weeping alone in the Hillhouse. . . . Bob Woodlee being lashed on a wagon wheel, while his parents screamed out their lives in a burning ranch house. He thought of the treacherous Nita Dell, who lured men to their death at Kyler Garriott's bidding. . . . Old Gurney sitting like a monarch behind that oaken desk. . . . The hideous-looking monster called Hodkey, and the tall, beak-faced, pockmarked Talboom. . . . The Delsings left on Wagon Mound with their son's grave and their home in embers.

When sleep did come to Cordell it was fitful, filled with fantastic and terrifying dreams, a whole world in flame and smoke, blazing furiously. Fever-heat scorched him, and gave way to freezing-cold horror. He was firing at Kyler and Gene, shooting straight through them without any effect at all, and they came on at him, laughing and mocking. . . . He was facing Hodkey and his gun-arm went numb, paralyzed, dead, so he couldn't lift his gun, and that frog-face was gibbering at him. . . . Then Cordell was drowning in a dark river of blood, and every time he clawed his way onto the slimy bank a great crippled boot stomped and trampled him back down into the vile torrent.

Progress the fourth day was painfully slow on the mountainside, but even then Chesbro and his reinforcements from Cadmus did not come up. Of all the trail-worn and nerve-fretted riders, Cordell was the most impatient and overwrought, sensing something portentous ahead.

"We're close now, Cord," remarked Andruss, pulling up beside him on the steep rocky trail. "I got a feelin' we're comin' close."

Cordell nodded. "I can feel it, too."

The sun was sinking in a western sea of flames over the distant Madrelinos when the trail narrowed into an even steeper rock-sided passage. After halting for a discussion, they left the trail and swung off to the left, climbing in a wide circle through a thinly wooded park of ash and laurel. Emerging finally on the rimrock, they dismounted and stared out over a long, narrow, crescent-shaped valley, with a stream curling along it like a slender ribbon of silver, and cattle grazing along the low flat banks.

Tannehill and Woodlee exchanged significant glances, and turned to Cordell. Ash was standing like a man turned to stone, only his gray eyes alive and shining, brimming with awe and wonder, as if at the sight of some fabulous and incredible vision. At the far north end of the crescent stood a great lofty butte, spired, pinnacled and arched like a vast cathedral of solid rock. The setting sun splashed its massive bulk with magnificent colors and shades, crimson and gold, blue and gray, purple and lavender, in all variations and blends. His eyes fixed on that stark grandeur, Ash Cordell was like a man standing before a shrine, after a long weary pilgrimage.

The base of the butte was shrouded with white mist from a waterfall. There could be no mistake this time. After all these years, Ash Cordell had come back at last to the valley of his childhood. Tannehill and Woodlee needed no words to confirm their first impression. A glance at Cordell's face was enough.

Near the center of the valley, about where the Cordell cabin had been, stood a large square blockhouse built of logs, surrounded by smaller shacks, sheds and corrals. The presence of sixty or seventy horses indicated a formidable force of at least fifty men in this mountain stronghold, and there must have been several thousand head of cattle.

"You'll find every brand in the whole Carikaree down there," said old Pruett, tugging at his gray mustache.

Men with field glasses were trying to identify the Hatchet hands moving about the expansive layout, and Cordell joined them in the effort. But even with binoculars it was difficult in the fading light, at that long range, although a few observers declared they had glimpsed Hodkey and Talboom, and others thought they had made out Kyler Garriott with his bodyguards, Red Hamrick and Pretty Boy Laidlaw.

"The two I want," whispered Bob Woodlee. "Those last two."

"You don't want to be hoggish, Woody," drawled Tannehill. "Give me one of 'em, won't you?"

Withdrawing to a spot well below the canyon rim, the posse made camp and warmed up a supper from their scant dwindling rations. Afterward a council of war was held about the low-burning fire. There was nothing to do until Chesbro arrived with his rear guard, but they should be along by tomorrow, at the latest. As Rubeling remarked:

"A sheriff's badge ain't goin' to mean a thing up here. We've got to have the manpower to back it up, that's all, boys."

There was no argument against this obvious truth, but Cordell said: "I'd like to drop down there tonight and scout around a little, Rube. Maybe find out who's there, and how many of 'em."

"It's pretty risky, Ash, and you might give us away," Rubeling protested. "You're just hungry to get at Kyler and the rest of them."

"I won't take any chances, Rube, and I won't start anythin'," Cordell persisted quietly. "I've got reasons of my own for wantin' to go."

"Could a man ask what they are, Ash? You're no way obliged to tell, of course."

"No harm in tellin'—now. This is the valley we

lived in when I was a kid. The valley my folks were murdered in, Rube. I've been lookin' for it all my life."

"Fire and damnation!" Rubeling said softly. "Then you've been right about the Garriotts all along, Ash."

"Looks like it," Cordell said quietly. "Good enough for me anyway, Rube."

"Well, go ahead, Ash," said the sheriff. "Just be careful, that's all. We're goin' to need you and your guns plenty, Ash."

"Reckon I better drift along with you, Cord," drawled Tannehill. "Kinda keep you out of trouble down there."

"Not this time, Tan," Cordell told him. "This one's better alone. I will take a chew off that plug of yours, though."

Ash bit off a chew, pulled on his buckskin jacket against the night cold of the mountains, gave a casual salute, and walked out of the ruddy firelight up toward the rim overlooking the valley.

Rubeling stared after him, his eagle eyes troubled. "Even Ash Cordell can't lick an army," he grumbled, shaking his high head.

"Maybe not," grinned Tannehill. "But Cord can sure cut a big hole in any army the Garriotts have got."

Down on the canyon floor in the misty moonlight, the night had an unreal dreamlike quality for

Ash Cordell. The moon, nearly at the full, was like a great searchlight flooding the earth, except when scudding clouds temporarily obscured it. Cordell had thought and dreamed so much of this moment that the actual discovery was almost anticlimactic. It had come about in the natural course of events, and there was an inevitability about it that made all his previous searching seem pointless and wasted. More and more Cordell was becoming a fatalist. He should have known that his destiny would lead him back here, sooner or later. He could have saved himself a lot of misery, fretting and railing and brooding.

After leaving the steep cliff and the talus slopes, it was easy going in the blunt wooded hillocks that rolled in gentle descent to the bottomland. Moving in the shadow of laurels and ash, pine and poplars, Cordell came close to the point where he and Sue Ellen and Clement had fled to rest and witness the burning of the cabin. Crouching there and watching the blockhouse, Cordell felt as if he were on hallowed ground that had fallen into enemy hands.

Hatchet men were sitting and lying about outside campfires, and some of their faces were clearly discernible in the wavering ruby firelight, but he recognized none of the leaders he was seeking. There were about sixty in the camp, he estimated, perhaps more with the ones that were already sleeping. In the loghouse men were

161

playing cards by lamplight, and he scanned their faces and forms through the broad window, with no better results. Neither Kyler nor Gene Garriott was in sight, and he failed to see anything of Laidlaw and Hamrick, Talboom and Hodkey. They could be there, of course, but not mingling with the rank and file.

What Cordell wanted was to get one of them off by himself where he could make the man talk, beat the truth out of him with a gun barrel if necessary. It was too much to hope for, he supposed. Apparently Gene hadn't brought Sue Ellen to this mountain refuge, and if Kyler and his two shadows had been in on the Delsing raid, they might have left the party for another hiding place. They could have doubled back toward Cadmus Flats or Hatchet, for that matter. Cordell went cold all over, thinking that Laura might be in Kyler's hands at this very minute.

Well, at any rate, Cordell had learned the answer to the question that had tortured and driven him through all the years of his life. The presence of Hatchet in Cathedral Valley indicated beyond any reasonable doubt that the Garriotts had been responsible for the murder of his mother and father. The fact that they had converted the valley into a holding ground for rustled cattle was sufficient evidence. The motivation behind the crime was a mystery that Cordell meant to solve. There was some link between the Cordells and the Garriotts which had caused Gurney to offer them shelter on Hatchet. Ash recalled the portrait of Gurney's uncle, to whom he bore a marked resemblance. A blood relationship there some-where, without a doubt.

He was about to withdraw when a hoarse voice bawled out: "Where's that durn Hodkey? He owes me ten dollars!"

There was laughter, and Cordell barely caught the words: "Down by the Falls."

Without waiting for any more, Cordell dropped back into the brush and trees, skirting the block-house widely and hiking toward the waterfall at the north end of the crescent-shaped trough. Cathedral Butte was a towering mass of mist-wreathed silver in the moonlight as he walked toward it, his mother's palace of splendor. . . . If he could catch Hodkey alone, and by surprise, Cordell would hammer him down with a gun barrel and make him talk. Hodkey had been Gurney's chief executioner for years. Hodkey must have been involved in the Cordell killings here, and he would know the story behind the deed.

Cordell increased his long swift strides, keeping to the shadowy edge of the glassland, warming his gun-handles with his palms and loosening the .44's in their sheaths as he walked. An upward glance at the Big Dipper told him it was about ten o'clock. Cattle raised their heads to gaze at him, their eyes large and luminous in the moonbeams, and Cordell noticed some of the brands. Old Pruett had been right: there were cows from every spread in the Carikaree. The smooth incessant roar of the waterfall was louder, and the shifting vapors thickened as he approached it. The moonlight was going to be tricky, with all that mist from the falls whirling and drifting about. In compensation, the thunder of the cataract would drown out any sounds of fighting, even to gunshots.

A cloud blotted out the moon and became rimmed with white fire, as Cordell threaded his way across a cedar-grown ridge and stood surveying the broad barren ledge that overlooked the waterfall. He had come there as a child, with his mother and father and the other children, to stare in awed tremulous delight at the mighty two-hundred-foot falls. Somewhere in the dense fog that blanketed the stone shelf Hodkey must be standing. Cordell crept carefully down the slope, a fine spray dampening his face, that steady endless roar in his ears. The moon sailed clear of the cloud, pure and serene, but there was still no sign of life on the level open ledge. Alert and keyed high, Cordell waited with tension growing in him.

The vapors swirled and interwove, then lifted momentarily, and Cordell caught a brief flash of a dark misshapen bulk on that terrace before the mists closed in again. There was no mistaking that wide squat ugliness, hunched with power and menace. Stepping forward, Cordell began to stalk Hodkey in the thick white fumes that rose and writhed, dipped and circled in an eerie fashion.

No sound could have been heard through the rush of water, but some uncanny animal instinct must have warned Hodkey of another's presence, for his shouting voice tore the haze: "Who's there? Is it you, Tal? Speak up, man! Who is it?"

Something prompted Ash to answer, and he yelled back: "It's Cordell, and I'm wearin' my gun-belt for you, Hodkey!"

"What?" The involuntary word was followed by weird laughter. "Cordell, huh? So you saved me the trouble of runnin' you down, boy?"

"Keep talkin', Hodkey. Tell me about killin' my father and mother in this valley, seventeen years ago. Tell me why Gurney wanted them dead!"

"You're ravin' crazy, son. I don't know what you're talkin' about. Let's get outa this fog and settle this right, Cordell."

"What's the matter with this? We both got the same chance."

"But you got a gun in your hand, boy," Hodkey accused him.

"Not me," Cordell replied. "I don't need any start, Hodkey. I'll take you from an even break."

"Good boy! We'll draw when the mist opens up, Cord."

"Fair enough." Cordell was straining his eyes, but the weaving gray veil was impenetrable. The minutes stretched on unbearably, and the blindness was maddening, intolerable.

A sudden narrow rift cleared between them, a radiant lane of moonlight, and both men leaped into their draw, shifting as they threw their guns level. The muzzle blasts stabbed out instantaneously, almost meeting and merging between them, the explosions felt as much as heard in the torrential downpour of the cascade. Cordell sensed the searing closeness of a bullet, and knew they both had missed. The murk settled back around them before they could fire again. The interminable waiting and stalking went on in that dense damp pall.

But one thing stood out in Cordell's frozen mind. That instant of clarity had shown him Hodkey's monstrous form lurching sidewise, vivid as a figure caught in a flare of lightning, dragging one leg in an awkward crippled manner. And on that foot was a clumsy grotesque boot, with a thick built-up sole and heel. "So you're the cripple, Hodkey!" cried Cordell hoarsely. "I saw that boot the day you shot my father and mother!"

Hodkey came in an abrupt limping charge through the gloom, nearly catching Cordell off balance and unready, but Ash was springing aside when Hodkey's gun flared. As Hodkey lumbered past, Cordell slashed his gun barrel viciously across that huge evil head, beating the man down onto his hands and knees. Ash drove in to smash the steel barrel home again, but Hodkey was rolling and thrashing away on the stone surface. Fire speared up from him, and Cordell felt the scorching breath of another slug as he let go again, the flame splitting the fog in a downward slant, the lead screeching off rock.

The haze rolled around them, denser than ever, and the deadly game of hide-and-seek went on in the ghastly swirling grayness. Once more the mist thinned out with magic suddenness, and this time Cordell was a shade swifter, thumbing off a shot before Hodkey could line his gun. The impact turned Hodkey, jolting him back toward the outer edge of the shelf. His right shoulder sagged, the arm dangling limp and useless, the gun dropping from the numb fingers.

Hodkey reached left-handed for his other holster, but Cordell's Colt flamed again. Hodkey buckled and reeled from the shocking smash of the .44, sprawling backward and scrabbling feebly on the ledge, a squat and shattered hulk. The fog stayed away longer now, and the terrace glittered in the moonlight as Cordell walked forward, eyes sweeping from that crippled foot to the froglike face, with its squashed nose, shark's mouth, and hooded eyes. Hodkey was dying, sobbing out blood with every groaning breath, unable to stir the gun in his large left hand.

"You'll talk now," Ash Cordell said, poised over him with gun barrel lifted to strike. "Tell me who my folks were, why Garriott had them killed. Talk, Hodkey!"

"Talk, man?" gasped Hodkey. "I'm—dead!"

Cordell straightened with a sigh. Hodkey heaved into convulsive action, threshing and floundering toward the brink of the chasm. Ash jumped to restrain him, but the crippled gunman was gone with an insane gurgle of laughter, falling over the rocky rim and vanishing into the misty darkness. The thunderous fall of water obscured any sounds his body might have made on the rocks and shale hundreds of feet below.

Turning away from the cliff as the white clouds surged in once more, Ash Cordell tasted sweat and powdersmoke on his lips, and found that he was soaking wet and quivering all over from the prolonged stress and strain. Hodkey was dead and gone, but Ash had learned nothing outside of the fact that Hodkey was the cripple who had killed, or supervised the killing, of his mother and father. Well, that score was settled, at least. Getting rid of a murderer like Hodkey was a good night's work for any man, but Cordell felt no exultation and little satisfaction.

There were still the three Garriotts left alive—Gurney and Kyler and Gene. There was still a great deal more to be done.

He wondered why Hodkey had hurled himself

over the cliff. To keep from talking maybe? Or because he didn't want anybody to see him dead from a gun-fight? Pride was a strong element in a professional killer like Hodkey. Well, it didn't matter, so long as the crippled brute was dead. Cordell was curious as to how the other Hatchet riders would take it. They had come to believe he was invincible, that Hodkey, impervious to danger and death.

Climbing through the cedars to the ridgetop, Cordell shucked the empties out of the cylinder of his right-hand gun and reloaded. The sweat, cooling quickly on his body, left him chilled and shivering in the cold night air. The moon emerged from another cloudbank and revealed three men walking down the river-side toward the falls, and he wondered if they could have heard the shooting, after all. He thought one of them was Talboom. They wouldn't find Hodkey, but they might discover his guns on the stone platform. That should tell them Hodkey was dead, and cause considerable fear and consternation among the Hatchet hands.

It might put some of them to flight, but Cordell hoped not. He wanted them all bottled up there tomorrow when the big posse came up. Now it was time for him to travel. Striding swiftly and hugging the western wall of the valley, Cordell headed back the way he had come.

Chapter XII

In the morning it seemed that at least half the Hatchet horses and men were gone. Apparently the crew that had participated in the raid on the Delsings, alarmed by Hodkey's disappearance, had moved out sometime during the night. Perhaps they had been able to see Hodkey's body at the bottom of the cliff. Anyway, they were gone, and the remaining riders were gathering the cattle, getting ready to drive them toward the main pass at the southern tip of the crescent.

Deputy Chesbro arrived to report that his posse would be along in about an hour. He had brought a force of twenty-five men. They would have made it yesterday, if darkness hadn't overtaken them. He also reported that the Delsings had reached Chimney Rocks safely, Dan was recovering well, and by this time they were probably in Cadmus Flats. But Chesbro knew nothing of the whereabouts of Gene Garriott and Sue Ellen Cordell, although he'd heard it rumored that they were going to get married. And he had no news of Kyler Garriott, Laidlaw and Hamrick. . . . The Hatchet bunch that pulled out in the night must have taken another route, because Chesbro's outfit had not seen them on the trail.

"They're gettin' set to move that herd out," Cordell said.

Rubeling nodded. "Ches, you drop back and bring up that posse as fast as you can. We'll be waitin' for you near the top of the pass. We've got men enough now to take what they got left here."

Chesbro started back down-mountain, and the rest of them finished saddling up and packing their gear in the cold-misted morning, gulping down scalding hot coffee about the small campfire. Cordell shaped and lighted a cigarette, sauntering alongside the sheriff.

"A few of us ought to work the inside, Rube," he said. "I found a way we can get horses down, and I figured to take Tan and Woody with me. If they start drivin' before the posse gets up, we could maybe head 'em off or slow 'em up some."

"All right, Ash, you three boys do that," Rubeling agreed. "If you want more help, say the word."

"I think three's about right," Cordell said. "Some of these horses wouldn't take to the way down I got in mind. I know what these three of ours can do."

"Good enough, Ash. We'll swing down around into the main trail."

"Get up to the head of it as soon as you can, Rube."

The Hatchet riders below were still rounding

up cattle when Cordell and his two companions reached the rimrock. Ash pointed out the precarious path down the cliffs, a narrow slanting shelf that switched back and forth across the rock face. It was slender and gradual at the top, widening and steepening as it descended.

"Not as bad as it looks," Cordell said. "We can ride that drift the last half of the way, right down into the timber."

Cordell led the way on his rawboned blue roan with the gray mane and tail, urging him smoothly and surely down the slim treacherous shelf, "Come on, Blue; come on, boy." Bob Woodlee's bright chestnut mare, borrowed from the Hillhouse stable, followed next, picking her way daintily and skittishly, not caring much for it. Tannehill brought up the rear, his tough wiry buckskin taking it in easy strides.

The ledge slanted first to the left, then to the right in a sharper but wider sweep, and back across the cliff to the left, ending abruptly above a perpendicular plane of naked rock. At this drop-off point, the shelf was wide and level, and Cordell waited there for the others. The early sun was crimsoning the eastern skyline above the Big Barrancas, and horses and men were already sweating. Woodlee looked up at craggy heights that reared above the timberline, and shook his head. "Some country—and you can have it," he murmured.

Below them, to the left of the vertical wall, was a soft shaly drift of gravel and talus rock, fanning out down the cliff and into the treetops, that seemed almost directly beneath the riders. Cordell stroked his mount's slate-colored neck, and jumped the gelding out and down into the precipitous chute. The dust smoked up as they slid downward with the surging soil, the blue roan wallowing deep and plunging his hoofs to keep abreast of the small avalanche they created.

Woodlee grinned at Tannehill. "This may be fun, but I'll take mine in a nice cozy saloon somewhere." He had to use the spurs before the chest-nut would take the leap, and Woodlee nearly went over her head when she landed, but the little mare straightened out and reared back valiantly, to ride out the deluge of dirt and shale, pitching and skidding with increased momentum into the delta at the bottom.

Tannehill kneed his mottled buckskin forward, drawling, "Take off, Bucky boy; ain't no little mare goin' to show you up here." The gelding jumped out, strong and fearless, riding the dusty torrent of earth and stones down, plowing powerfully to keep from being swamped, rocketing the last thirty feet in a straight breathtaking plunge, coming out of it squarely on all four feet, and shaking himself clean of the clinging dirt.

Dismounting in the trees, they cleaned out under their saddle blankets and double-rigged cinches, examining their horses' hoofs and legs for possible injuries from the shale. Back in the leather again, they traversed sparsely forested hills toward the bottle-neck entrance at the south end of the canyon, watching the open grasslands where the herd was being gathered and formed for the drive.

"If they start runnin' 'em now, we've got to turn them," Cordell said grimly. "Our bunch won't be up for half an hour or more."

"Sure looks like they're fixin' to start," said Tannehill, glancing uneasily toward the deep sharp cleft that marked the passage in the rocky walls.

A rifle shot sounded from the heights over that natural gateway, and at this signal the Hatchet cowhands set the herd in motion, Talboom building and stringing out his point, the swing riders yipping and yelling on the flanks, and others pushing and prodding in the dust of the drag. "Come on, boys!" Cordell said, and the three riders flattened their horses into a headlong run down the edge of thc valley floor. If they didn't turn that point, the herd would be in the notch before Rubeling's crew ever got there to blockade it.

"Fire and pitchforks!" Cordell cried suddenly. "They aren't drivin' that herd; they're stampedin' it!" He realized then that the lookout on the heights had seen the posse in the narrow cut below, and Hatchet meant to stampede the steers down on top of them. It was instantly and vividly gruesome in his mind, what a floodtide of berserk beef would do to Rubeling's party, trapped in that sharp, steep, rockbound defile. . . . Urging Blue into a reckless gallop, Cordell lifted his carbine out of the saddle sheath and levered a shell into the chamber. Hammering wildly along in his wake, Tannehill and Woodlee did likewise with their rifles.

Talboom and his Hatchet men were howling and whooping like Apaches, lashing ropes and quirts at the heads and flanks of the cows, and firing into the air to complete the panic. Talboom had pulled off the point now, the lead steers bolting in a maddened rush for that cleft in the wall, the other crazed creatures thundering after them in the boiling dust. The ground trembled under thousands of beating hoofs.

Cordell opened fire at the dead run on the nearest swing riders, with Tannehill and Woodlee chiming in with their carbines. One Hatchet horse and rider went barreling down in the clouding haze, and the others swung around to return the shots, lead singing and whining on the morning air. A running fight developed, with a lot of racket but little damage done, as there was no chance for accurate shooting with both sides at a full gallop. The stampede was on in all its terrible unleashed fury, a veritable avalanche of cattle roaring toward the pass and shaking the earth beneath it, dust storming high and red in the early sunlight. It had all the primitive violence of a hurricane.

Cordell led the way in a final desperate drive to reach the point, head off and swing the frenzied brutes, but the distance was too great, the time too short, the momentum of the herd unstoppable. There was nothing to do but fire into the lead steers and attempt to turn them that way. Converging on the point near the open gateway, they emptied their carbines into it. Steers fell and rolled under hammering hoofs, but the herd bucked and surged on over the fallen, stomping them to jelly and pouring on unchecked, a solid roaring river of beef flowing into that steep-sided passage, making the ground shudder under its thunderous power and might.

Pulling up and out of the brawling ruck, Cordell and his mates dismounted on a boulder-strewn shoulder close above the pass, their six-guns blazing steadily as they fired into the rush of cattle. But there was no stopping it. A ragged barrier of dead and dying animals blocked the way, but the herd tramped over them and swept on with irresistible force and speed. Rubeling and his men were lost, if they were caught on that narrow trail below.

They reloaded quickly, and barely in time, for Talboom was leading a Hatchet charge at their position, and bullets were already screaming and ricocheting all about them. Talboom, tall and beak-faced in the saddle, with four horsemen at his heels, hurtling in at them with guns aflame. Cordell lined his carbine and squeezed off a swift shot, and Talboom flew from his horse's back, long arms and legs awry, dead before he bounced on the sunbaked sod.

Tannehill and Woodlee made their shots count, spilling two more of the enemy riders, and the other two whirled and fled, hanging low on their ponies' necks. Tan and Woody switched their aim back into the torrent of beef. Cordell was lunging at a large boulder balanced on the rim of the ledge, directly over the pass. Laying his shoulder into it, driving hard with his booted feet, Ash heaved all his strength against the stone. It gave slowly, tottering, toppling at last, crushing a steer's back as it settled ponderously into the corridor. Cutting loose both his Colts then, Cordell rejoined his comrades, who were sill blasting away steadily. Gradually, as dead cattle piled up higher and higher around that boulder, a dam was formed, solid and lofty enough to check the stampede finally, turn the herd into a milling, slowing circle.

But more than enough cattle had gone through to obliterate a posse down there in the gulch.

Loading their heated guns once more, Cordell, Tannehill and Woodlee turned their sweat-shining, powder-streaked faces to look for trouble up the valley. They had done their best, but Ash feared it wasn't good enough to save Rubeling and the rest.

Hatchet seemed to be through fighting, withdrawing toward the shadow of Cathedral Butte at the north end, leaving four dead men and a few dead horses on the plain. But there were more slain steers than anything else.

Sheriff Rubeling, riding with his deputies at the head of the column, was nearly up to the valley entrance when the rushing trample of thousands of hoofs first reached him, the shooting broke out above, and the herd hit the pass like a tremendous avalanche.

"Ride or climb for it, men!" shouted Rubeling, but there was little time or room for either.

The posse was hopelessly trapped in the deep, narrow, stone-walled cut, with that oncoming mass of horned beef bearing down on them with stunning speed and suddenness. Rubeling knew dread and horror as never before. The front riders had no choice but to try the sides. Those in the rear had some chance in flight.

Horses snorting and pitching in panic, the riders wheeled and scattered before that berserk juggernaut of beef. Rubeling drove his red roan at an almost sheer wall, with scrubby trees overhanging it from a ledge about thirty feet up. The great steed responded superbly, powering up somehow high enough so Rubeling could catch a handful of tough gnarled branches. For a blood-freezing moment, Rubeling was hanging in midair, and then he hauled himself onto the shelf, struggling and straining with a strength born of fear and desperation. The horse planted his hoofs deep in a shaly spot and clung flattened there on the wall, ears flat and eyes rolling in terror. Getting his gun out, Rubeling started shooting into the boiling stream of cattle below.

Others were less fortunate than the sheriff. Chesbro's pinto, crazed with fright, reared high with pawing forelegs in the middle of the trail, and went shrieking over backward under the terrible onslaught, the paint horse and Chesbro both instantly buried under tons of beef. Old Pruett, the harness-maker, was hurled from his saddle and tossed from horned head to head, bouncing and torn until he disappeared under the hoofs. Paynter's sorrel stumbled and fell in front of the lead steers, and Paynt tried to claw his way up a sheer stone wall but was brushed off like a fly, trampled immediately under. Dust geysered up in the channel, with the bawling of beasts and the screaming of men. Rubeling went on swearing and shooting into the rampaging herd.

Little Koney went for the same wall and ledge that Rubeling was on, kicking out of the stirrups and stretching up enough to clamp his fingers on the sharp rim, hanging there until Rube dragged him up to safety. Koney's bay gelding slid back and was lost in the torrential current of cattle, while Koney dropped panting on the shelf. "Too old—for this," he gasped. "Never goin'—to get out from—behind that bar again."

Deputies Maddern and Shokes were lucky enough to strike a slope of shale, and drive their mounts scrambling steeply up it and out of danger.

Those farther down the trail had a little more time to pick embankments their horses could climb, or to ride back to where the walls widened somewhat and there were zones of comparative safety off the trail. But not all of them escaped. Andruss, the man from Chimney Rocks, was pinned against a cliffside, crushed and ground to death with his mount. And Jencks, a hostler from the Riverside Corral in Cadmus, went down under the flying, stamping, pulverizing hoofs. Others would have died there, if the tide hadn't been stemmed by that blockade at the mouth of the pass above.

The rock-walled corridor was ghastly with dead men, horses and steers, reeking like a charnel-house, as the survivors crept back into the trail with frozen faces and shocked eyes. A glance was enough to ascertain that the five posse members were beyond any help. Rubeling led the remainder of his troop up the passageway, over a barricade of dead beef, and into the valley. Cordell, Tannehill and Woodlee were in full command there, the Hatchet hands having vanished at the far end of the crescent.

"Thank heaven," breathed Cordell, scanning the haunted faces. "We thought you were all gone down there. How many, Rube?"

"Five," Rubeling said, naming them off: "Chesbro, Paynter, Pruett, Andruss, and Jencks."

Ash Cordell shook his bared bronze head. "An awful price, Rube. This valley has always been a valley of death."

"It would've been worse, if you boys hadn't done a good job up here, Ash." Rubeling studied the heaped carcasses, the Hatchet corpses, and the herd that was grazing peacefully now. He swore softly. "Well, let's get this slaughterhouse cleaned up some."

Koney smiled sourly. "I ain't goin' to be much good at diggin' graves, Rube, until my stomach settles down some."

"We all need a break," Rubeling said, biting off a fresh chew of tobacco. "Anybody got any drinkin' liquor left in this outfit?"

A few bottles were produced and passed around, and the men rolled cigarettes or lighted their pipes.

"That Talboom out there?" Rubeling said thoughtfully. "Old Gurney's lost some of his best gunhands lately. Hodkey and Talboom here. Eakins and Blodwen in Scalplock Canyon. Thorner in Trelhaven, and Skowron'll never do any more gun-slingin' either. And he's goin' to lose some more. Old Gurney Garriott's got to the end of his road."

The tall sheriff turned his hawk-face on Cordell, the eagle eyes lighted. "You still want to be a deputy, Ash? I'm goin' to deputize the three of you, right here on the spot—Cordell, Tannehill and Woodlee. In force until Hatchet is smashed, the whole Garriott gang, every last devil of 'em! You got any hunches now, Ash, go ahead and play 'em."

"It'll look like we're tryin' to get out of the dirty work here, Rube," said Cordell with a sober smile. "But I think us three ought to hit for Cadmus. There's goin' to be a weddin' I want to go to, and I think Kyler's probably back around there with Laidlaw and Hamrick."

Rubelong pondered this briefly and nodded. "All right, Ash. You've got a right to handle that end of it, I reckon, and here's to a clean sweep. We'll be ridin' on Hatchet when we get through here. It's time for Gurney himself to pay up, too."

"Thanks, Rubc," said Cordell. "We'll see you back in the Flats."

The three mounted up again, waved in farewell, and clambered over the barrier of butchered stock, which was already swarming with flies and insects. Vultures were beginning to flap evilly overhead, as the trio of riders descended into the death-strewn corridor of stone.

Chapter XIII

They made fast time on the return trip, traveling alone and unencumbered, swapping horses at small ranches along the way. Everybody was talking about the war with Hatchet, and feeling was running higher than ever against the Garriotts. Every spread they stopped at was going to send men along when Rubeling came out of the Shellerdines to march on the home layout of old Gurney Garriott. The army that Cordell had visualized as being necessary to wipe out Hatchet was coming into existence at last. Rubeling would have more than enough manpower to overrun the decimated Garriott forces.

Riding day and night, with only a few hours' sleep in every twenty-four, Ash Cordell lost track of time, the days, and everything except the urgent driving need to get to Cadmus Flats before Sue Ellen could marry Gene Garriott. The first thing he meant to do was break up that affair. Secondly, he had to run down Kyler Garriott, the murderer of his brother Clem, and with him Pretty Boy Laidlaw and Red Hamrick. After that, the prospects were more pleasant, involving Laura Delsing and another marriage that Cordell intended to consummate.

It was evening when they came in along Bittersweet Creek and saw the lights of Cadmus glimmering hazily across the Carikaree River. North Bridge boomed hollowly beneath their horses' hoofs, and then they cut across Western Avenue into an area of back yards and lots, to approach the natural terrace of Hillhouse Hotel from the rear. If Kyler and his two gun-sharps were in town, they might be watching the hotel and waiting for an opportunity to drygulch Cordell and his friends.

But they reached the stable without incident, and climbed down, weary and stiff with saddle-cramp, turning their spent horses over to old Zach, the night hostler.

"Better saddle up some fresh ones, boys," suggested Cordell. "I'll go in and see what's cookin' in Cadmus. Ma must have heard from Sue Ellen before now."

"Bring back a bottle," Tannehill sighed. "I never needed stimulants so much in my life as I do right now."

"Bring two, Cord," said Bob Woodlee. "It'll take plenty firewater to keep me awake and movin' tonight."

Ma Muller was still at work in the kitchen, cleaning up for the night, her tired face and faded blue eyes lighting up at the sight of Cordell, disreputable-looking as he was. His hard angular face, bristling with a bronze stubble of beard, black with powder, alkali and dirt, had aged and hollowed in the past week. His clothes were sweated out, brush-torn, filthy and drenched with dust.

"Thank heaven you're back safe, Ash boy," she said. "How did it go, after you left the Delsings?"

Cordell told her, tersely and concisely. Then his gray eyes narrowed intently on her. "Where is she, Ma? Where's Sue Ellen?"

"How would I know where anybody is, Ash?" she sputtered. "I never step a foot out of this kitchen. I—"

"You know, Ma," he interrupted quietly. "Tell me now."

Ma Muller sat down quickly, heavily, as if her legs would no longer support her weight. Resting her elbows on the table, she held her broad face in her veined hands. "I don't know, Ash. I just don't know where the girl is."

"The Delsings still in town?"

"Yes, they're here in the hotel. Dan's comin' along fine. Laura, of course, has been worryin' herself sick."

"Any other news, Ma?"

"I hear Kyler Garriott's back here, with Hamrick and Laidlaw."

"That's good. Now tell me about Sue Ellen. You're an awful poor liar, Ma." Cordell smiled gently, and stroked her bent gray head.

"Ash, I can't," she mumbled through her

fingers. "I can't tell you, Ash; you've got to leave them alone. Kill Kyler, if you must, but let Sue have Gene. It's all she wants in this world. Please, Ash boy, *please!*"

"The Garriotts had our folks murdered, Ma. I'd rather see Sue Ellen dead than with one of them!"

"Gene didn't do it, Ash. Gene never killed anybody. He's a good boy, Ash. He'll make Sue a good husband."

"He's a Garriott," said Cordell coldly. "That's enough. Where are they, Ma? They're around here somewhere, I know they are. You'd better tell me the truth."

Ma Muller moaned and let her arms fall helplessly on the table, a martyred look of anguish on her face. "In the church, Ash," she said, her lips scarcely moving. "They're gettin' married— tonight." She laughed with a bitter sound. "Tonight, of all nights! Couldn't you have stayed away a few more hours, Ash?"

"It wouldn't make any difference, Ma. I'd never let her stay married to a Garriott." He touched her silvered head tenderly and slammed out the door, holding down on his guns as he ran for the stable, thinking of the day he had found Clem practicing his draw out there.

Tannehill and Woodlee had the fresh horses saddled, and were slumped down in exhaustion on bales of hay in the corner, while old Zach rubbed down the trail-worn animals. They looked up, scowling when they saw Cordell empty-handed.

"Just in time for the weddin', boys," Cordell told them. "Our three friends are in town, too. The drink'll have to wait a little."

Groaning, they stepped into leather and loped toward the front of Hillhouse, pausing for a moment before the gallery. Front Street lay straight beneath them, quiet at this end, loud and gaudy in its remote reaches. The church spire showed white and thin over the outer portion of Court Street. Cordell swung his hand, and they dropped down the grade and across Western Avenue at a gallop, the remounts strong and lively between their thighs.

They were drawing abreast of the adobe bank building on the corner of Court Street when flames split the night with a roar, leaping out from the far corner of Murphy's Market across the way on their left. Bullets hummed close and screeched off adobe as they threw their horses into the nearest right-hand alley.

"Cord, you better get on to the church," drawled Tannehill. "Woody and I'll handle this here."

"Sure, Ash," said Woodlee. "We'll take care of this end of it."

Cordell thought it over quickly. "Well, this is one weddin' I sure don't want to be late for, boys." Wheeling his horse, he drove back the length of the alley and out across back yards into Court Street. Shots rang after him as he lined out past the courthouse toward the church at the far end.

While the snipers were shooting at Cordell, Tannehill and Woodlee dashed their mounts straight across Front Street and swung down in the shelter of the near wall of Murphy's Market.

"I'll circle around back and smoke 'em out, Tan," said Bob Woodlee. "I figure these are my two boys."

"Leave me one of 'em, Woody," drawled Tannehill. "If I can't drink, I want to fight."

Woodlee mounted again and rode toward the rear of the huge store, while Tannehill peeped around the front corner. Wisps of smoke curled from the alley at the other end of Murphy's, but that was all. This part of the town seemed empty and deserted. Down at the east end, there were racked horses, wagons, and riders and pedestrians were milling about in the yellow light of kerosene flares and lamps. Koney's Longhorn and other saloons, the Golden Wheel and the Rio Belle were doing a brisk business as usual. The saddle and harness shop of old Pruett, dead up there in the Shellerdines, looked desolate and dark. Tannehill hefted his Colt .44 and waited, his long frame loose and easy, hoping they were up against Laidlaw and Hamrick, and he would get a fair crack at one or the other.

Bob Woodlee, alert in the saddle, drifted through back yard darkness at the rear of the market, gun balanced in his right hand, as he held the nervous horse in with his left. A blinding explosion all but scorched his eyeballs and set the gray gelding to rearing and pitching as Woodlee fired back, having glimpsed the pretty girlish features of Laidlaw in the muzzle-light.

But Laidlaw was gone, whipping into a narrow aperture between two low sheds, legging it out toward the deeper back lots and the river. Quieting the horse, Woodlee sidled him against one of the shacks, freed his boots from the stirrups, and hoisted himself onto the flat roof. Racing back along the rooftop, he saw that the slender passage between the walls was vacant now.

At the rear of the roof, Woodlee flung himself flat as roaring fire burst upward at him from a huddle of ashcans and rubbish barrels. Crawling closer to the edge, Woodlee tilted his gun down and turned loose a couple of shots, the recoils jerking his wrist. The slugs screamed off metal and Laidlaw was moving again, running toward the Riverside Corral.

Woodlee left the roof in a reckless leap and took after the baby-faced killer, heedless of everything but running him down. Flame torched back at him again and something smashed him to a sudden, stumbling halt, his left shoulder numbed by a terrific sledging blow. Woodlee went down on hands and knees in the thin grass, rolling desper-ately as fire licked toward him again. Spotting the dim shadowy outline of Laidlaw's graceful dodging figure, Woodlee raised his Colt, lined it steady, and triggered. The Pretty Boy was down now, gasping and threshing in the weeds, and Bob Woodlee smiled as he crept forward, the pain breaking through the numbness and squeezing the sweat out all over him in large drops.

Laidlaw was hard hit, dying, when Woodlee reached him, no longer pretty with his eyes bulging and his mouth distorted, but still trying to get his gun up. "Remember up on the Bittersweet?" panted Woodlee. "Remember how you laughed, Laidlaw?" Laughing weakly himself, Bob Woodlee hammered his gun barrel down across that twisted sweating face, and Laidlaw screamed through the blood, "No, *no!*" Woodlee said, "Laugh, Pretty Boy, laugh!" and he struck again with the steel barrel, feeling the bones of the face give in under it. Laidlaw's last scream was soundless behind that bloody ruined mask as he slumped back, still and dead in the dusty weeds.

Satisfied and too tired to care much about anything else, Bob Woodlee dropped wearily beside him. . . .

Tannehill, hearing the gunfire out back and seeing nobody emerge in the street, turned and ran toward the rear of the alley, coming out into the cluttered dimness and rubble of the back yard just as the broad massive bulk of Red Hamrick appeared at the far back corner of Murphy's

Market. They fired almost simultaneously. Tannehill, ducking away from a vicious spray of splinters, saw Hamrick jerk and stiffen as the lead struck him. But the great bull of a man held his feet, leaning back against the loading platform of the store, shooting again as Tannehill stalked toward him, window glass breaking somewhere on Tan's right with a crashing jangle.

Still walking forward with long, easy, loping strides, Tannehill brought his gun level and fired twice, the bright flashes stabbing out through the shadows, tearing Hamrick away from the wood, spinning him in slow backward circles, dropping him heavily into an absurdly awkward sitting position. Using both hands and groaning with the effort, Hamrick heaved his gun up, but the orange flame blossomed high into the air. Tannehill, slouching close now with limber effortless ease, threw down once more with his .44 Colt, the blast lighting Hamrick's ugly snarling face, rocking the red head, stretching him back full length in the dirt.

Tannehill looked down at him for a long moment, reloading his gun with deft automatic fingers. The shooting out toward the Carikaree had ceased some time ago. Tannehill spat on the ground, his lean face sharp and solemn with a yellow flare in the eyes, and walked on, a slim whiplash figure, to find Bob Woodlee.

Running footsteps pounded closer in the street,

but Tannehill paid no attention to them. A cool clean breeze from the river washed the cordite fumes out of his head. He hoped Woody was all right. They might make that wedding yet.

Chapter XIV

The whitewashed frame structure had been modeled after the old Colonial churches of New England. Severely simple and plain, with a square bell-tower surmounted by a graceful tapered spire, it had a clean austere beauty and dignity that was incongruous in a rude sprawling Southwestern town like Cadmus Flats. Tonight the church was lighted, but the tall stained windows permitted no view of the interior.

Ash Cordell left his horse at the hitch-rail on the side, and walked around to the front where the outer double doors were ajar. Stepping reluctantly into the vestibule, he moved stealthily to an inner doorway and peered into the main room, feeling like a shabby and guilty intruder.

Sue Ellen and Gene Garriott were standing before the altar, over which a black-garbed, cadaverous-faced minister presided. There were two old ladies in attendance, and apparently the ceremony was about to begin. Sue Ellen, her hair golden in the candlelight, was a pure lovely figure in her white gown. Gene looked tall, handsome and distinguished in a dark blue tailored suit. A fine-looking couple to the casual observer, but not to Ash Cordell. It wasn't much of a wedding, he thought. There was something hasty and furtive about it.

Cordell didn't like this breaking into a religious service, but there was no other way to stop it. Suddenly and painfully conscious of his dirty tattered clothing and grimy unshaven face, Cordell stepped inside and paced down the aisle, hat in left hand, his head tousled and sun-streaked in the flickering light. The parson stared aghast at him, until the others turned their startled faces. The elderly ladies looked ready to scream, and Sue Ellen seemed on the verge of fainting. Gene Garriott's fine carved face was suddenly murderous.

"Ash!" cried Sue Ellen. "Please, Ash, you know better than this!"

"Who is this man?" demanded the reverend.

"Her brother," Cordell said. "I've got a right to be here. Sorry, folks, but there isn't goin' to be any weddin'. I'm a deputy sheriff too, and I'm arrestin' Gene Garriott."

"For what?" Gene asked disgustedly. "You're crazy, Ash. Get out of here and leave us alone, you fool!"

"You're wanted, Gene. All you Garriotts are

wanted. For murder, cattle rustlin', and other things. Come on, Gene; I'm takin' you."

"I wish I had a gun on me!"

"You'd still come, gun or no gun. Come on; I don't want to rough you up in church."

The minister raised his hand. "Young man, you are desecrating the House of God!" he declared in sonorous pulpit tones.

Cordell smiled gravely. "Any house with a Garriott in it is desecrated. Come on out with me, Gene."

Gene Garriott glared around in helpless rage. Sue Ellen had collapsed sobbing into a front pew, and the old ladies were striving to console her, from time to time darting fearful scathing glances at Cordell and his two holstered guns. The parson stood with his hands folded, a severe wrathful look frozen on his gaunt pale face.

Cordell strode forward and clutched Gene's arm. Garriott wrenched violently away from him. Ash drew his right-hand gun and jabbed the muzzle into the big man's ribs. "Outside, Gene, or I'll bend this iron over your head!" Garriott gestured despairingly and started up the aisle, with Cordell walking after him, sheathing the gun. The faint broken sobbing of Sue Ellen followed them into the vestibule, and there Ash closed the door on it and motioned Gene outside.

In the front yard, they stood staring at one

another with that bone-deep lifelong hatred springing from innermost depths into their eyes. Cordell was ragged and filthy, in contrast to Garriott's groomed elegance.

"We found Hodkey's valley in the Shellerdines where you hide the stolen cattle, Gene," said Cordell evenly. "The same valley where Gurney had my father and mother killed, seventeen years back."

"I don't know a thing about that, Ash."

"Hatchet burned the Delsings out and killed young Fritz, up on Wagon Mound. Just like they burned the Woodlees out five or six years ago, only they burned Mr. and Mrs. Woodlee with the place."

"I had nothing to do with either of those cases," Gene said. "I never took part in any of those things, and you know it, Ash."

"All right, then," Cordell said. "Tell me about my mother and father."

"I don't know anything about it."

Cordell smiled thinly. "Well, you're a Garriott. You might as well die with the rest of 'em."

"I haven't got a gun, Ash," protested Gene.

"Here's one!" Cordell drew his left-hand gun and tossed it on the sun-dried lawn near Gene's highly polished boots. "Pick it up, Gene. I won't make a move until you get hold of it. See?" He held his open hands spread shoulder-high.

Gene Garriott looked from the gun at his feet

to Cordell, and back again to the revolver. Cordell stood motionless, lithe and easy, hands level with his wide shoulders. Gene slid his boots apart and bent his knees slightly, crouching, gauging distances and perspectives, nerving himself for the vital daring move.

"No, I won't do it," he muttered.

"You'll either reach, or talk," Cordell told him. "It's a lot easier and safer to talk, Gene."

"I've got nothing to say to you."

"Look, Hatchet's busted. You Garriotts are all through runnin' the Carikaree. Gurney's got nothin' left, not even a prayer. You won't be givin' anybody away, Gene."

Gene crouched a trifle lower. "I won't talk. And this isn't an even break on the draw, Ash."

"It is with my hands up here," Cordell said. "I won't move until your hand is on the gun."

"It still isn't a fair chance."

"Quit cryin'," Cordell said. "It's more of a chance than Clem had. Or my father and mother. Or young Fritz Delsing. And hundreds of others. Reach before I beat your head in!"

Gene Garriott's hand went to the gun on the grass like a striking snake, and Cordell's right hand streaked down from its shoulder-high position as Gene's fingers closed on the grounded weapon. Cordell's Colt flashed clear and blazed first, and Gene's exploded into the turf as the slug shattered his forearm. Dirt spattered across Ash's legs, and Gene let go of the gun as blood coursed down, dripping from his fingers.

The minister appeared in the church door. Cordell waved his .44 at him, saying: "Get back inside. Nobody's hurt here—yet." The white face vanished at once.

Gene straightened up slowly, holding his broken right arm across his waistline, supported by his left hand. Staring down at it, he shook his head, the black curls falling picturesquely on his glistening wet forehead. After a while Gene looked up at Cordell.

"All right, Ash. Go ahead and shoot."

"I want to find out a few things first, Gene. What's the connection between your family and mine?"

Garriott laughed contemptuously. "Connection? Why, nothing, except we took you in and gave you a home. Fed you, clothed you, educated you, brought you up decent. And all we get from you is *this!*"

"Talk straight, or I'll beat it out of you! Wasn't my mother a Garriott?"

Gene tried to sneer. "I hardly think so! Go ahead, kill me."

"If I wanted to kill you, you'd be dead now. Or long before now," Ash Cordell said. "I just want to hear the truth, Gene. And you want to live and marry Sue Ellen, don't you? All you've got to do is talk a little. Didn't Hatchet belong to my mother once?"

"You *are* crazy!"

Cordell clipped him across the head with his gun barrel. Gene dropped to his knees, groaning and swaying, curly head bowed and blood trickling down his handsome face.

"Talk, blast you!" grated Cordell. "We're cousins, aren't we? Second cousins, I mean."

"All right, I'll talk," Gene Garriott panted, wiping the blood from his eyes with his left hand. "Yes, we're second cousins. Your mother was Gurney's first cousin. She inherited Hatchet, but—"

"When she married my father, Gurney drove her out," Cordell finished tautly. "When Gurney found them up in the Shellerdines, he had them both killed. Isn't that right, Gene?"

The kneeling man nodded. "Yes. I didn't know about it until Kyler told me once. Gurney didn't want me to know, said I was different." Gene looked up ferociously. "Come on; get it over with!"

"My grandfather was the brother of Gurncy's father," Cordell mused wonderingly. "I began to think when I saw that picture in the office at the Big House." Cordell pickcd the gun off the ground, sheathed both of them, and lifted Gene to his feet. "Go on in there and get married," he said. "If that's what Sue wants, it's good enough for me. And you aren't to blame for what Gurney and Kyler have done, Gene. Hurry up and get that arm to a doctor, boy."

Gene Garriott blinked disbelievingly at him, and then smiled. "You really mean it, Ash? Well, that's going to make it a lot better all around." Holding his broken arm across his chest, he walked toward the church entrance, pausing on the broad steps to say: "Sue Ellen's going to be very happy, Ash."

"I hope so," Cordell said, smiling back at him. "Tell that parson to come up to the Hillhouse when he gets through with you folks. I reckon he can stand two weddin's in one night."

Gene went inside the church, and Cordell stood gazing at it for an interval, deep in thought. At last he knew the whole story, in bare outline anyway, and it was as he had gradually come to formulate and believe it, in his mind. Then, remembering that Tannehill and Woodlee were in trouble on the other side of town, Cordell started toward the corner and his horse. He had one thing left to do before he could marry Laura Delsing, and that was to kill Kyler Garriot. He ought to cancel that order for the preacher, but he wasn't going back into that church tonight. Absently he replaced the spent shell.

Cordell was suddenly aware of rapidly onrushing hoofbeats, and a shot roared out from behind him, the bullet burring close and splintering the façade of the church. Spinning and drawing lightning fast, Ash saw a huge white horse hurtling straight in at him, looming gigantic in the vague light, and the flash of another shot speared toward him.

Quicker than thought, Cordell hit the turf in a flat headlong dive, sliding into the angle formed by the steps and the building itself, his head ramming solid wood with a stunning shock that jarred all the way to his flying bootheels. A slug ripped a shower of splinters from the stairs, as the white horse thundered past. Cordell glimpsed a black-garbed lanky figure in the saddle, and knew it was Kyler Garriott. The last big showdown was at hand, and Ash was lucky to have lived through this much of it. Kyler must have been awfully overanxious to miss three times like that, even if he was on a galloping steed.

Twisting around in the grass, shaking his head to clear the aching haze, Cordell fired from the ground just as the white horse made a rearing starfishing turn. The shot struck that high silvery body, and the horse screamed with a horrid human note, fell floundering backward in the swirling dust. Kyler Garriott flung himself clear of the leather, and lighted catlike on his feet in the shadow of the great gnarled live oak beyond the church.

Cordell was up by that time, striding forward with gun in hand, and Kyler came out to meet him, a towering black figure that blended into the dark background, while Cordell was plainly silhouetted against the white church. They fired almost together, the flames lashing out brilliant and loud, and Cordell felt the hot lead fan his cheek, as Kyler staggered slightly with dust puffing from his black shirt.

Thumbing the hammer swiftly, Cordell lined his Colt and let go another shot, the slug slamming Kyler into a back-tracking teeter, his right hand jerking high as the gun went off, the bullet clanging the bell in the church tower. Shot through twice, Kyler Garriott was still on his feet, lurching but upright, trying to level his right-hand gun and draw left-handed at the same time.

But Ash Cordell, swinging into a balanced crouch, had freed his trigger finger and was fanning the hammer with the heel of his left palm now, the .44 held firmly in the right, bucking with each bellowing roar, three swift shots blazing and blending into one tremendous sustained blast. Kyler Garriott blundered backward, jolted by each successive smash, until he bounced from the trunk of the live oak, twirled in a foolish, flop-armed, jack-kneed arc, and toppled slowly at last in a long stilted stagger, his snarling coyote face rooting the earth.

Turning wearily and walking back toward the church, the empty gun hanging loosely in his hand, Cordell was dully surprised to see a small crowd of men gathered there, afoot and on horseback, and among them the tall whiplike leanness of Tannehill.

"He sure took a lot of killin', Tan," said Cordell. "Where's Woody?"

"Caught one in the shoulder, Cord, but he'll be all right," Tannehill said. "He got Laidlaw and I took Hamrick. So this just about winds it up."

"And high time, Tanny," murmured Cordell, shaking his sweaty bronze head.

Tannehill looked at the lighted church windows. "What about the weddin', Cord?"

"It's goin' on. I got the story out of Gene, and I sent him back in to Sue Ellen." Cordell smiled wryly. "That's what she wants, and I guess Gene's all right. I've busted up enough things anyway."

"So you know the story, Cord? But you don't know the endin'." Tannehill's smile was bright and boyish. "Some riders just came in from Hatchet. Old Gurney's gone too, Cord. Shot himself when he heard what happened up in the Shellerdines, and found out that Rube was headin' his way with the biggest posse this country ever saw."

Cordell regarded him with mild wonder. "Old Gurney, too? Well, that does wind it up."

"Gurney left a letter before he swallowed that gun muzzle," Tannehill drawled on tantalizingly. "Right interestin', that letter, so they say. A full confession, you might call it."

"That so?" Cordell was trying to taper up a

smoke with fingers that felt thick and numb, and he didn't seem unduly interested.

"Yeah, quite a thing," Tannehill went on, undaunted. "They tell me, Cord, you've got yourself a ranch. The biggest spread in these parts."

Cordell laid a long arm on Tannehill's rangy shoulders. "Reckon I've got me a foreman, too. And we'll have a pretty fair tophand when Woody's shoulder gets healed. Now I've got to see about gettin' a woman to keep house, I suppose."

A hand plucked at Cordell's ragged shirt-sleeve, and a soft familiar voice said: "That shouldn't be very hard for a man like you, Ash. Especially with those whiskers, and the way you dress."

Then Laura Delsing was in his arms, her mouth reaching eagerly up to his, heedless of the beard-stubble and powder-grime. "You wouldn't marry a man that looks like this, would you?" Cordell asked.

"Why, sure," Laura smiled, imitating the way Ash said it. "As long as you're going to own the biggest ranch in the Carikaree."

"Well, one thing is sure," drawled Tannehill, grinning and scratching his own rusty whiskers. "You'll have the best-lookin' best man in this valley, and that's whatever."

"At Hillhouse we can wash, change, and get that drink we missed," Cordell suggested.

"Why not hit this preacher when he's all set up for business?" inquired Tannehill.

"He's comin' up to the hotel later," Cordell said, still holding Laura and breathing in the sweet clean smell of her.

"Nothin' like confidence!" marveled Tannehill, laughing. "This Cord's up against the fastest gun in the country, and he ain't even asked the girl. But that don't stop him from orderin' up a parson!"

About the Author

Roe Richmond was born Roaldus Frederick Richmond in Barton, Vermont. Following graduation from the University of Michigan in 1933, Richmond found jobs scarce and turned to writing sports stories for the magazine market. In the 1930s he played semi-professional baseball and worked as a sports editor on a newspaper. After the Second World War, Richmond turned to Western fiction and his name was frequently showcased on such magazines as *Star Western*, *Dime Western*, and *Max Brand's Western Magazine*. His first Western novel, *Conestoga Cowboy*, was published in 1949. As a Western writer, Richmond's career falls into two periods. In the 1950s, Richmond published ten Western novels and among these are his most notable work, *Mojave Guns* (1952), *Death Rides the Dondrino* (1954), *Wyoming Way* (1958), and in 1961 *The Wild Breed*. Nearly an eighteen-year hiatus followed during which Richmond worked as copy editor and proofreader for a typesetting company. Following his retirement, he resumed writing. Greg Tobin, an editor at Belmont Tower, encouraged Richmond to create the Lash

Lashtrow Western series. In these original paperback novels, Richmond was accustomed to go back and rework short novels about Jim Hatfield that he had written for *Texas Rangers* magazine in the 1950s. When Tobin became an editor at Bantam Books, he reprinted most of Richmond's early novels in paperback and a collection of his magazine fiction, *Hang Your Guns High!* (1987). Richmond's Western fiction is notable for his awareness of human sexuality in the lives of his characters and there is a gritty realism to his portraits of frontier life.

Center Point Large Print
600 Brooks Road / PO Box 1
Thorndike ME 04986-0001 USA

(207) 568-3717

US & Canada:
1 800 929-9108
www.centerpointlargeprint.com